EAGLE ROCK
117 DAYS OF LOSS, FEAR AND SURVIVAL

BY
RAENETTE PALMER

EAGLE ROCK
117 DAYS OF LOSS, FEAR AND SURVIVAL

BY
RAENETTE PALMER

Running Dog Studio
175 Liza Lane ~ Commerce, MI 48382
raenettepalmer@yahoo.com ~ www.running-dog-studio.com

ISBN 978-0-9815635-0-3

Santa Quits also written by Raenette Palmer

Dedication

There are many people who helped in the evolution of this book. Dozens of teachers read it to their classes and offered feedback. My own third and fourth grade classes were enthusiastic editors. Friends and family never failed with encouragement and love. One friend, Peggy Kraemer, went above and beyond with her editing expertise. Thank you Peggy! My husband, Steve remains my greatest admirer and the love of my life. Without him none of what I do makes as much sense.

PART ONE
- Loss -

Chapter 1
June 25, Day 8

Ryan woke from a dreamless sleep. He opened his eyes and was instantly awake and anxious for the day ahead of him. He looked over at Ben sleeping like an Egyptian prince in his mummy bag and gauged the time to be around 6:00 a.m. He pulled his hand out of his sleeping bag to see how close his guess was. He pressed the button to illuminate the dial and saw it was 6:08 and smiled. Guessing time was a game the twins played with each other ever since they'd been old enough to tell time.

Ryan lay still and listened for sounds; he heard wind whispering through pines, birds waking up in the hills, bugs buzzing around the tent, and the snoring of Ben. He liked this solitary feeling. Back home in New York they lived in a crowded neighborhood close to an expressway so it never got this still. He rolled over, closed his eyes and tried to get cozy but his eyes popped right back open. It was no use something called him outside. He slipped out of his sleeping bag. He already had on a flannel shirt and socks. He tugged on his jeans then reached for his boots with his left hand while unzipping the tent door with his right. Sticking his head out the flap he glanced over at his parent's tent. Sensing no movement he crawled out and sat down to lace up his boots.

He felt powerful being so high up in the Appalachian Mountains, alone except for his sleeping family. He stretched and bent over a few times to get the kinks out, and then he saw it, an eagle! Once he straightened up and reoriented himself he saw it again. He almost shouted for his

Dad and then thought better of it. *Our first eagle! After more than a week of searching I found it.* Ryan hadn't really cared one way or another about the eagle's nesting place until now. Admiring the bird, gliding overhead, he was overcome with an urge to find Eagle Rock and give it to his dad as a present. Without thinking he began to move with the eagle, keeping it always in sight. *The nest, or the aerie, as dad calls it, can't be far.* He'd find it and then go back to get his family.

Ryan ran through some woods, around a pond where his family had collected water, and into another opening. The eagle swooped and landed on a branch at the top of a tree. Ryan caught his breath and reached for his compass to take a reading. That's when he realized he hadn't put on his survival vest. He needed to make a quick decision; run back and get the vest and risk losing the eagle and waking up Ben; or go on to find the nest himself. The eagle flapped his wings and was on the move. Ryan moved too. He knew his mom would be furious but she'd get over it, in the meantime he might lose the eagle if he went back to the tent. The eagle dipped and glided, all the while leading Ryan, he was sure, to its aerie. He didn't stop to think that each step also brought him farther from the safety of his family.

He had to run fast now, going up and down smaller hills and in and out of thickets. His breathing was labored, his mouth felt dry, and he remembered he hadn't brushed his teeth. He took a quick look around to mentally map the way he'd come. There weren't any clear landmarks but he was sure he could find his way back. As he turned to look up at the eagle his foot caught on the root of a scrub pine and he went down. When he fell he hit a patch of loose shale and began to slip. He slid sideways toward the edge of a ravine hitting rocks, weeds, and sticks. Gnarled roots grabbed out for him and he tried grabbing back, but couldn't manage to catch one. His mouth was dry, his throat hurt, and he realized he was screaming. With a thud that rattled his body, he crashed into a tree growing at an angle from the mountain. The screaming stopped as his breath was knocked out of him. The abrupt halt caused him to bite down hard, shooting pains through his head and clacking his teeth together. He lay there wrapped around the tree gasping to catch his breath. Rocks fell around him, hitting his head, legs and back on their way down the mountain. He became aware of blood dripping from his forehead and momentarily wondered if he had any loose teeth.

After several minutes Ryan began to breathe normally and rolled onto his back, still using the tree as a brace. It hurt to move so he stopped and started several times before he found a position he could tolerate. He stayed this way, staring into the sky and waiting until his head cleared and the sky stopped swirling. He wiped at his forehead with his shirtsleeve. Raising his arm cut pains through his chest and the movement nearly made him black out. Tears flowed down his cheeks and his mind called out to his parents, just as it had every time he'd gotten hurt in the last thirteen years. He wanted them to find him, and make it better. The rational part of him knew he couldn't lie there waiting for this to happen, but the thought of trying to make his way up the mountainside exhausted him. *You are so dumb! Dumb! Dumb! Dumb!*

After a few seconds he quit whining and gritted his teeth, which shot new pains through his head. His tongue darted around checking for something loose inside his mouth, but he couldn't tell. He inched his way up the tree so he could take better stock of himself and his surroundings. Each movement took forever and seared his chest with pain. It was hard for him to move and breathe at the same time. After many tortured minutes he was able to lean against the tree at a strange angle, not quite sitting up and not lying over either. He looked up, but the eagle was nowhere in sight, scared off by the noise. He risked a look over one shoulder and panicked when he saw how much farther down he would have fallen if this tree hadn't stopped him. The steep incline below had only loose pieces of shale and an occasional mountain laurel. He froze when he realized there still wasn't any guarantee he wouldn't slide further down if he weren't careful. This thought paralyzed him.

Ryan hadn't felt this alone or scared for a long time. He wanted to cry and scream for his dad, but besides being too far away for anyone to hear him, he was hurting too badly to cry anymore. He brought his watch up to check the time. He'd been following the eagle, at a good trot but he couldn't believe it was already 7:12 a.m.

As his head cleared he began to feel aches and pains in different places on his body. The gash on his forehead was still wet with blood. His jeans were ripped just above the left knee and blood was soaking the area around the hole. Seeing his own blood made him panic. He started breathing heavily and couldn't get his mind off thoughts of falling farther down; of not being able to move; of wild animals smelling his blood and tracking him. He tried thinking of his twin, channeling energy in a more positive direction and this dug something from his memory. When he and Ben were nine years old they were in a soccer tournament. An opponent tripped Ben and his brother fell, hitting his head on a rock. By the time Ryan and his dad got to him, blood was pouring down Ben's face. Ryan started crying, afraid for his twin, until the coach reassured him that cuts to the head always resulted in a lot of blood. At the hospital, after Ben was cleaned up he didn't even need stitches, just a couple butterfly bandages.

Ryan lifted his right arm to wipe more of the blood away on his sleeve but his breath caught when his arm was partway to his forehead so he put it back down. He scolded himself, *don't be a baby. You can't just sit here not moving and expect to be found.* With new resolve he held his breath and dabbed at the cut on his forehead. His sleeve came away bright red.

I've got to move. If I have a broken rib it's not going to kill me, but if I stay here against this tree who knows what will happen? Ryan looked around, planning the best way to get back up to flatter ground. He focused on a few exposed roots and some scrub pines about a foot off to his right. *That's the way to go.* With difficulty he managed to get down on his hands and knees with his butt against the tree. He couldn't put much weight on his left knee, but his ribs hurt less in this position. He gave himself a moment to try and take a deep a breath. In truth he was breathing shallowly protecting himself from a fractured rib pressing against his lung. Ryan inched his way from the relative safety of the tree to a tangle of roots and smaller scrub trees.

Trying to ignore the pain, he grabbed hold of the sturdiest looking trunk and pulled himself up to a kneeling position. "There, that wasn't so bad," he said out loud to encourage himself. The sound of his voice scared a bird nesting nearby. The loud 'caw' stretched Ryan's nerves tighter and he let out a scream, which echoed over and over down the mountainside. Listening to that echo made him realize how alone he really was.

"It was just a crow you idiot! Get going! Freaking out won't help anything." Ryan talked out loud again as he began his slow ascent. Each move he made hurt something on his body. The cut near his knee was particularly brutal as he crawled and stretched. He winced every time he hit a piece of rock or weed. Ryan wouldn't let himself look down, it only made things worse to see how far down it really was.

The shale that had given him trouble when he fell was even worse on the way up. He used roots, rocks, and even sturdy looking weeds to steady himself. For each yard he made, he slipped back a foot. He stopped often to rest and gasp for air. He was crying and didn't even realize it. Ryan reminded himself to keep his mouth closed to help moisten his throat so he could swallow easier, but the mucus in his nose prevented him from breathing normally for long. The cut on his forehead was throbbing and blood dripped into his eye making it hard to see. The story of Hansel and Gretel leaving breadcrumbs to mark a trail flew through his mind and he gave a chuckle wishing he had either Hansel or Gretel with him now. *I'd even take the witch,* he thought and then let out a sob. "Big baby!" he called himself out loud, "get going. Just do it!"

On one of his frequent stops he thought of last summer, when his parents had taken Ben and him to The Mall of America in Minnesota. At that time it was the biggest mall in the world and even had an indoor amusement

6

park and rock-climbing walls. He and Ben climbed that wall over and over, racing each other to the top. His dad told them that real mountain climbing was much more strenuous. *Right again Dad,* he thought.

As if mocking him for getting lost, an eagle reappeared and circled overhead. Ryan paused, gasping for breath. He wished he had woken his family to go with him, but no, he'd wanted all the glory of finding a nest. This burst of anger got him going a few more feet.

After another rest, where he allowed his body to stretch fully out, belly on the mountain, hands wrapped securely around a root, and feet digging in as best they could, he began climbing again, still chastising himself for his stupidity. He knew he deserved any punishment, which might come his way once he made it back to camp. His mind drifted even further from immediate danger and pain to how happy he'd be to see Ben and his parents. Then he slipped again. He grabbed at the same plants he'd just used to help him up and caught one. He felt a root slice into his fingers but continued to hang on. His toes and knees dug into rocks to keep him from slipping. He wanted to direct himself out loud but couldn't manage the breath so he thought it instead. *Concentrate Ryan. You can daydream all you want later, but there won't be any later if you don't make it to the top! Now get your left hand up to that weed. Test it for strength.* He began moving again. *That's it, now move your right arm, forget about the pain, you can cry later. Move the left foot now. You got a good hold there so keep going with the left arm.*

Ryan crawled the last yards to the top and wasn't sure what hurt most, his head, ribs, hands or knee. With a

7

sigh of relief he lay down on secure ground. Every inch of his body felt like it was on fire. He began to shake and finally let the tears flow freely. After a few minutes he was cried out, and decided he'd give anything for some tissues and water. His eyes felt itchy and puffy and he knew he should move farther away from the ravine, but it felt so good to be safe that he allowed himself a few extra minutes of stillness.

Slowly he got to his hands and knees and then even made it to his feet, shaky, but ready to head back to camp and face the music. He looked around and saw trees and boulders, grass, weeds, clouds, and birds, but nothing that looked familiar. Through the fuzz in his head he tried to remember looking around and keeping track of where he'd been running when he was following the eagle, but everything looked the same. One tree looked just as green or sparse as another. There was no clear opening for him to head into, no trail, nothing that jogged his memory, and with a rising sense of panic he realized he wasn't sure how to get back to camp. "Okay," he said aloud to control his fear, "Think. What did Dad say to do in a situation like this? Check your compass – I blew that piece of advice." His voice was barely audible but it made him feel better to hear it. "Next, he said to keep an eye out for mountain cats and bears so you don't stumble into their territory. Great! This all looks like their territory much more than it looks like mine! He also said to drink plenty of water to keep from getting dehydrated. That's not gonna happen either since I didn't bring my canteen." This morning's idea of following the eagle seemed like a really stupid one and he wondered how it could have gone so wrong?

Still talking out loud he began to take stock, once again, of his cuts and bruises. His head had finally quit bleeding but his face felt itchy and pulled in an unnatural way from the drying blood. Crying cleared the blood from his eye, but gnats were buzzing around his head and sticking to it. His knee, which was covered with dirt, had stopped bleeding. His hands were cut and swollen from grabbing at roots, and his chest ached when he breathed deeply or moved certain ways. He was sure he'd broken one of his ribs. The rest of his pains were from bumps, scrapes, and scratches. Ryan thought he'd be even more bruised tomorrow, but all in all he felt lucky to get away with the injuries he thought he had and hoped his dad wouldn't cancel the rest of the trip because of him.

He turned his attention back to orienting himself, straining his eyes for a slight trail he might have made following the eagle. He knew he'd run out of a thicket toward a crevasse, but which thicket? Which crevasse? There was nothing that looked anymore familiar than anything else, and a new surge of panic shot through him. He had no idea where he was, or in which direction he should go.

Ryan looked up at the sky hoping to see the eagle, just to make a connection with something alive. As he gazed upwards he turned in a full circle, making him lose his balance. He fell down hard, feeling hungry, thirsty and light-headed. There was no eagle in sight, and the clouds dotting the sky held no more clues than the ground.

He leaned against a tree and closed his eyes. Images of his mom and dad and Ben surfaced. *They must be frantic,* he thought. He cupped his hands and shouted their names, straining his already sore throat and chest. He continued shouting, but his voice was nothing like the loud, strong cry he wanted. Ryan kept at it until he could shout no more and then sat and listened. The only answer he got was the grumbling of his stomach. He checked his watch. It was 8:17 a.m. but his body felt like it had been up for days. Next he examined his leg. The dirt and gravel had formed a bandage over his cut, but he knew when he started walking again it would open back up. For now he left it alone.

As he attempted to decide what to do, Ryan asked himself if it was better to stay put in one place and wait to be found, or better to pick a way and start walking? He weighed the pros and cons, and wondered what his dad or Ben would do in this situation. Resting in the warm sun and trying to think made him sleepy.

The adrenaline, which kept him moving before was spent, and Ryan's body began to relax bringing on an exhaustion he'd never known before. As the sun dried the sweat on his body he could hardly keep his eyes open. *I'll just rest a minute,* he thought as his eyes closed.

He was in the middle of a dream about the Mall of America. He and Ben were at the indoor amusement park riding a huge eagle around. Just as they were dipping toward an Old Navy store, a strange sound woke him. His heart thudded against his ribcage so hard he knew if someone had been looking they could have seen it jumping through his shirt. He lay still for a moment, not sure where he was and why he hurt so much, but listening for the sound that woke him. The heat of the sun on his exposed skin made it feel like mid-day. *How long have I been sleeping,* he wondered as he opened his eyes. Then he heard it again; a growl that sounded like an angry cat, but much, much louder. He twisted his throbbing head trying to locate where the threatening sound was coming from. The gash on his forehead reopened and fresh blood seeped from the wound.

Chapter 2
Camp – 8:10 a.m.

At 8:10 Ben rolled over in his sleeping bag. He'd been dreaming that his twin was in danger. He pictured Ryan in a clearing, paralyzed with fear. When he opened his eyes he tried to shake the dream from his mind and looked over at his brother's bag to see if he had woken up before him. As usual, Ryan was up first.

Ben scrambled out of his bag and grabbed for his jeans and boots. He got dressed in the tent and stepped outside. No sign of Ryan – or his parents – he noted, as he looked around the campsite. His parents were still sleeping. This would give him time to explore with Ryan. He scanned the campsite again for his brother, and then assuming he was off at the latrine, headed in that direction.

After Ben finished using the hand-dug bathroom and walked back to camp he still hadn't found Ryan. He looked inside their tent again but the two sleeping bags lay empty and rumpled. A wave of fear rippled through his body and images similar to his dream, sprang into his head. With that came the certainty that only identical twins feel - Ryan was in danger! He ran to his parent's tent and unzipped the door flap without even asking permission to come in. "Ryan's gone!" he screamed.

"What?" shouted his father sitting up and reaching for his shirt, all in one fluid motion.

"Ryan's gone Dad! I looked all around camp. He's not here!" Ben's voice cracked. He looked at his mom who had gone white and was sitting eerily still clutching the top of her sleeping bag with both hands.

His dad raced out of the tent, nearly knocking Ben over in the process. "Ryan! Ryan!" he shouted, cupping his hands. No answer. "Ryan! Ryan!" Still no answer. Ben remained crouched by his parent's tent, looking in at his mom.

"What's going on Ben," she said softly.

"I don't think he's anyplace he can hear us Mom. I think he's hurt. I don't know how badly, and he's scared."

"Anything else?"

"No, but these aren't good feelings!"

"It'll be okay," she comforted him, but there was no real conviction in her words. She listened to her husband shouting Ryan's name while she laced up her boots and brought out Ted's.

Ben went over to his Dad and said, "He can't hear you."

"What do you mean he can't hear me?"

"I mean he's too far away."

"You don't know that," his Dad countered. He always ignored his sons' ability to sense what was happening to the other. Sarah Burns felt differently. From the moment she knew she was having twins she read everything she could on the subject. Then, when her sons were born and they were identical, her reading time was consumed by books about identical twins. Sarah believed what Ben was saying. She had seen her boys be right about each other too many times not to believe him.

"He's hurt, Dad, but I don't know how bad, and he's really scared," Ben repeated.

Mr. Burns took his boots, absently tugging them on. "He'll be okay. He's got on his survival vest."

"No he doesn't."

"What? Can you sense that too?" his father railed at him.

Stinging from his dad's remark Ben shot back, "No, our tent still has two vests in it." Ben didn't even try to stop his tears this time. He just let them slide down his cheeks before wiping them away. Sarah gasped and grabbed her son's arm.

"Okay, we're not helping Ryan by any of this," said Ted. "Come here, both of you." Ben and Sarah moved toward him and he put his arms around them. "It'll be okay. I'll make it okay. I promise!" This time it was Ted whose voice cracked, but he regained control and said, "I think you should stay here Sarah. If Ryan comes back he may need some immediate care. Ben and I'll go searching for him. You with me Ben?"

"Sure, Dad."

"You okay by yourself Sarah?"

"Yes, just go find him! Bring him back!"

"Ben, get your vest. Sarah get my backpack and make sure we've got plenty of snack food, a couple space blankets, and water."

"You won't spend the night out there will you?"

"No, we'll be back before long. The blankets are just a precaution. If he's injured he may be in shock and we'll have to keep him warm."

Sarah left to get the supplies while Ted looked around the campsite for clues to which way Ryan may have gone. He could have set out in any direction and that thought alone nearly brought him to his knees. He saw Ben and Sarah looking to him for guidance so he grabbed the supplies from his wife and set out in the direction he was facing, which was the exact opposite of where Ryan had followed the eagle.

Starting off in this direction didn't feel right to Ben, who wanted to tell his dad, but the look on his dad's face kept him silent.

Chapter 3
Ryan – 2:00 p.m.

The growl sounded louder and more real than anything Ryan had ever heard come from TV. It reminded him of the lion-taming act in the circus and made the hairs on his arms stand up. In spite of the sun overhead he began to shiver. He was disoriented and couldn't tell exactly which direction the growling was coming from. He knew it had to be behind him because he saw nothing in front of him. Another roar echoed down the mountain. Ryan started to sweat and the saltiness of his sweat mixing with the dried blood on his face made him itch. He didn't turn around for fear the animal, whatever it was, would think he was challenging him. He knew some animals protected their territory fiercely. He also knew that the smell of blood brought carnivores around, and he had lots of blood on him.

Maybe it's a bear, Ryan thought to himself. *I could be between her and her cubs! I should move away. But if it's a mountain lion, I need to stay still.* He worried the animal could sense his weakness and he tried to calm himself down by thinking, *This doesn't happen to kids who are going into eighth grade, kids who play soccer, and get straight A's on their report cards.* He tried breathing evenly, forcing his heart to slow down and his body to stop shaking, but it was no use. The harder he tried the worse it got, and every time he heard another growl his fear ratcheted up a notch. He was paralyzed and couldn't remember anything his dad taught him about survival in the wild. Instinctively, he knew he needed to do something; just sitting wouldn't help.

16

He risked a painful look around his left shoulder. He saw a tree about twenty feet away. He knew the mountain continued up to his right. Straight ahead there was nothing but more trees and hills folding in on each other. It had to be coming from behind him toward his right. He whispered to himself, "Slowly, Ryan. Don't make any quick moves. Okay, that's it." He was barely talking out loud, but the sound of his own voice soothed him. "I'm such a jerk! Okay now that's it. A little bit further and you'll be able to see behind you. That's it. Slowly." He was panting shallowly and his body screamed for him to stop moving, but he managed to look over his right shoulder with his body turned halfway around. He saw a rock ledge jutting out the side of the mountain, about fifty feet away. On the rock, pacing back and forth, twitching its tail was a mountain lion, staring right at him.

Ryan didn't believe it was possible to feel anymore fear than what was coursing through his veins, but the look of that cat, all muscle and sinewy strength, let loose a new surge of anxiety. His breath caught in his throat. He turned his head back to face the trees in front of him. He could never outrun it, especially with the condition he was in. Climbing a tree was out of the question; he was already in such bad shape that the cat would get there before him, and could climb trees better anyway. *There's only one way out,* he thought, *back down the mountain and hope the cat doesn't follow. If I can back down a ways and come up someplace else, he'll realize I'm not a threat.*

From his sitting position, Ryan inched his back up the tree he'd been leaning against and then thought better of it. He needed to stay small. Every movement hurt and he didn't want to waste the energy he'd just used, but he realized he should crawl to the side of the mountain. He inched back down, feeling every cut and bruise on his body. The hurt rib made him almost cry out but he bit his lip and silenced himself. By the time he was sitting back down the cat was growling again. He forced himself up on his knees and crawled, head down, to the side of the ravine, praying all the way. It took every ounce of his courage, to keep his head down while he was turning around so he could back off the mountain. Eyes away from the lion, he lowered himself over the same precipice that just a few hours earlier he had worked his way up. He tried feeling around with each step making sure not to slip on any loose shale.

The cat watched all of this intently, twitching his tail, growling, and continuing to pace nervously.

Chapter 4
Ted and Ben

"What do you think Ben, does this way feel right?"
Ben took a few seconds before answering his dad, and tried
to connect with his twin. This was the third or fourth time
today his Dad had asked him this question. Ben knew his
father didn't believe in the connection he shared with Ryan,
and now, when so much rested on these feelings, Ben didn't
trust them either. So far he'd been unable to lead them to
Ryan. They'd walked over an hour before Ryan told his dad
he thought they were going in the wrong direction.
Reluctantly, his dad took them back to camp and they started
off in a different direction that felt better to Ben. But having
his dad rely on him for the first time was making him
nervous. They'd already been searching for hours and had
returned to camp twice throughout the day to check on Sarah
and make sure Ryan hadn't come back. Each time they tried
a new path but with no luck.

Ryan – 3:07 p.m.
About 20 feet down the ravine Ryan spotted a large
flattish rock off to his right and over about 10 feet. He made
his way to the rock an inch at a time. As he climbed toward
what he hoped was safe ground he listened for the cat, but
heard nothing. He was so tired that his body was shaking and
he was finally happy to have the solid ledge beneath his feet.
He knew he needed a rest before trying to make it back up
the mountain again and to his family. He wondered if he'd
gotten far enough away from the cat? Just because the

19

growling stopped didn't mean it was gone. *What if* he's *waiting for me when I come back up?* He decided he was safe for the moment so he laid his body down on the rock, back against the mountainside and closed his eyes.

Ryan – 4:58 p.m.

The screech of a bird jarred Ryan awake. He sat up quickly and regretted it. His head pounded, he was weak, hungry, and thirsty. He realized he was on a rock ledge and needed to move carefully. He wasn't sure how long he'd been asleep but his body seemed to crave it. He ached worse than before he fell asleep, and the bruises on his chest from where he hit the tree was making it harder to get a breath without sending pains through his lungs. He stayed still and listened. The wind sighed through the trees, crickets and cicadas and birds were winding up, but he heard no growl. Since the sun was no longer visible overhead he knew he needed to get off this rock and back to his family before it got any later.

He panicked when he saw how small the rock was. It had looked big and safe earlier. At a snail's pace he turned around to face the mountainside and look for a place to get a foothold. The panic he felt shot adrenaline through his system, giving him enough energy to get to his knees. He reached above his head and gasped when pain shot into his lungs and his cries rolled down the mountain. Ryan wanted to collapse but he reached with his other hand and gritted his teeth against the pain as he got hold of a root. His hands were already cut and swollen making grasping painful. With each foot he gained he hung on to the side of the mountain panting and hoping his Dad or Ben would walk by and hear him. He was getting used to the razor-like pains in his chest, but his jaw was aching from clamping it shut. His knee was throbbing and his head felt like it belonged on someone else's body.

Peeking over the edge of the mount he saw nothing menacing, and pulled himself onto more solid ground. He lay face down in the dirt, breathing in its comforting safety. His body felt good lying there, not hanging on and grasping for the next foothold. The cramps in his hands and feet began to relax. He looked at his watch 5:42 p.m. *Now what do I do? Stay here and wait to be found, or start walking again?* He realized this was the same question he'd posed to himself before he encountered the mountain lion. After he rested a while he dragged himself to his feet, cupped his hands and tried shouting for his family. After all he'd gone through, without any food or water since last night, the shout wouldn't rise above a whisper. He waited - no answer; he didn't really expect one, but it disappointed him.

Mosquitoes and gnats decided to make his face their evening meal and he didn't have the energy to swat them away. At least there was no growl. He still wasn't sure what to do so he sat back down at the base of a tree and listened to a different growling – that of his stomach. He felt light-headed and hot. He couldn't manage to keep his eyes open and when he closed them he was out instantly.

7:39 p.m.

Ted didn't want to leave Sarah alone any longer. Night was falling and he felt a need to gather his remaining family in one spot, but Ben wasn't ready to give up.

21

"Ryan's out there somewhere Dad. I know he's not back at camp with Mom, I wish I'd get a lead on which way to go." His words sounded hollow to him. "I'm sorry."

Mr. Burns shook his head. "Don't worry about it. We need to get back to Mom." He stopped and checked his compass then turned them in the direction of the campsite. "We need more help and we're hours away from the tents." Ted was not looking forward to returning without Ryan.

8:10 p.m.

When Ryan awoke his face was in the grass and he didn't know where he was. Panic shot through him and he tried to stand up. The aches and pains kept him riveted to the ground. He tried again, this time taking things slowly, and managed to stand. The world spun around him and if he'd had anything to throw up he would have gladly done it to stop the nausea.

It was getting dark and Ryan realized with a look at his watch that he'd been gone about 14 hours. The lack of food and water, the exertion of the day, and his injuries, especially the blow he'd taken to his head, made it hard to think clearly. He wondered if it would be better to wait until morning or to keep going? *Why do I keep coming up with the same question?* He thought he remembered a full moon from last night when he and Ben stayed up long past their parents and tried to scare each other with ghost stories around a dying fire. He couldn't believe that was last night. It seemed like an eternity ago.

He looked up, and there it was, a full moon against a darkening sky. *It could help lead my way tonight, but which way? One thing's for sure, I'm getting nowhere staying here!*

"I'm dying of thirst!" he said aloud, just to test his surroundings, but no animals rustled. He reminded himself that he could very well die of thirst if he didn't get moving. With that thought he dragged himself a few feet and gingerly tried to stretch his aching body.

Chapter 5
Camp – 10:03 p.m.

Sarah was pacing outside the tent when she heard branches breaking. "Ryan?" she called out as she ran, feeling sure this time he'd be returning with Ben and Ted. But the fire she'd started hours ago, hoping the smoke or smell would help guide her son back, served only to illuminate the despair on the faces of her husband and Ben. "NO!" she cried. Why are you here if you don't have Ryan?" Ben winced at the shrill sound of his mother's voice.

"We'll find him honey, just not today. It's dark and we need help." Ted put his arm around his wife before he spoke again. "I'm leaving now before it gets later. I should be back to the car by tomorrow early in the morning. We'll get trackers and dogs up here. We *are* going to find him Sarah!"

Tears streamed down his wife's face and ran off the webbing of her survival vest. She was still shaking her head as she turned back toward the campfire. Ben caught up with her and slipped his hand inside hers but she barely noticed. They watched Ted restock his backpack. "How will you find your way in the dark?" Ben asked.

"There's a full moon tonight and I've got my compass and the log I've been keeping. Don't worry about me watch out for each other. I'll be back tomorrow with help." His words were meant to reassure his wife and son, but they didn't. Ted gave them each a kiss and headed off. Sarah was numb, she couldn't believe it would be hours before the search continued, and she toyed with the idea of leaving Ben at camp and going out on her own to look for Ryan. Instead, she watched Ted retreat until Ben interrupted her thoughts.

"Come on, Mom," he said. "Sit closer by the fire with me. You look cold." Sarah allowed herself to be steered to a log. Ben threw some sticks on the embers. With that task done he looked at his mom for comfort, but the only light he saw in her eyes was the reflection of the flames.

Chapter 6

Ryan began walking straight ahead. He had no idea if it was the way to go, but he needed to move and it was as good as any other way. Besides, he needed to find water. The full moon provided light, but his movements were slow and labored. It hurt to walk, and he couldn't take a breath without pain. He found himself breathing shallowly, which didn't help his light-headedness and he had a headache that wouldn't quit.

He needed something to lean on to help bear his weight. *A walking stick,* he thought. After minutes of searching the ground he found an adequate branch and stripped off the limbs, all the while wishing he had the pocketknife that was in his survival vest. Even this amount of activity sapped Ryan of his failing strength and he needed to rest before trying out the walking stick.

Through trial and error he found that prodding the ground in front of him first, with the stick in his right hand, and then leading with his right side he could pull his left leg forward without bending it. The gash at the knee had stopped bleeding and he didn't want to reopen it. Movement was so slow he measured his progress in feet and yards.

He could keep his mind off the pain in his body only by concentrating on getting back to camp, but nothing let him ignore his dry mouth. It was so parched that swallowing was an automatic reaction, giving him no relief. Every night sound intensified the realization of how alone he was. A hooting owl became a sinister fiend asking Ryan, "Whoooo, whoooo, whoooo are you to be in these mountains?" The wind whistled a tune through the trees and Ryan's mind put words to that too, "Gooooo baaaaack, goooo baaaaack!" Bats flapped overhead and occasionally darted to catch an insect.

At the best of times Ryan didn't like the dark, but he had the comfort of Ben for company. To keep his spirits up, and to give himself some company he began to talk out loud pretending his twin was there with him. "It's okay Ben, we'll find our way back. Dad's out looking for us right now. Everything's going to be okay. We need to keep moving. I know you're tired and hungry but we'll have plenty to eat and drink as soon as we get back to camp. Just keep moving." By the time Ryan had convinced himself that things might be okay, the wind whipped up around him. This time it was harder and lashed the trees back and forth, creating the same eerie, but more insistent warnings he'd heard earlier, "Goooo baaaack! Goooo baaaack!"

Camp – Midnight

"Ben, wake up!" cried Sarah, shaking him in his Dad's sleeping bag. "Did you hear that?"

"What mom?" asked Ben, feeling guilty for sleeping. As soon as he closed his mouth he heard it too, a scratching outside the tent. His mom started for the door flap and Ben broke out in a cold sweat watching her unzip it. Hadn't he promised his dad he'd watch over her? "I'll go Mom," he said, touching her on the shoulder. She was relieved and moved back into the warmth of her bag. She handed him a flashlight near the top of her pillow.

The scratching grew louder and faster, and Ben thought of the story he liked to tell Ryan of the dead hand scratching at people's car doors to get in. It took all his courage to peek out. *Was it Ryan too weak to shout for help? Was it a wild animal eager for fresh meat? Was it the hand?* He moved the light one way and then the other. He couldn't see anything unusual so he ventured further out, crawling on his hands and knees. The light bounced ahead of him illuminating shapes in the distance.

"What is it?" he heard his mom whisper from inside the tent. Just then, a family of raccoons scurried away from the other tent, two young ones tumbling over each other and a larger one, the mother, hurrying them along with her nose. Ben let out a high-pitched laugh; more from relief than thinking it was funny.

"It's just raccoons, mom. I forgot to close up our tent. They're probably after the food in Ryan's pack." He was sorry he'd said it as soon as it came out but it was too late. His mom was already out of the tent. He saw her brush away tears from her face.

"I'll go zip up the tent." He raced the ten yards and carelessly pulled up the zipper. He'd been in too much of a hurry and it caught the screen at the bottom, where it began to curve. He sat down to free it, tugging first one way and then the other, while the flashlight jostled in his lap. He was so intent on getting back to his mom and the relative safety of their sleeping bags, that he didn't hear the buck approaching from the back of his tent.

His nerves were strung as tight as a rubber band. The buck surprised him and he let out a scream causing the buck to bolt back into the thicket and his mom to come running, screaming his name. "I'm fine Mom, just got spooked by a buck," he said shakily.

Seeing what Ben was trying to do she reached down and helped him free the screen. "I don't expect you to take care of me, Ben. We need to take care of each other. We could be in for a long night," she said, noticing the trees swaying. "It looks like a storm is brewing." Ben sighed, talking to his mom helped ease the knot in his stomach. Unfortunately, just as quickly as it eased, he thought of Ryan out in a storm, alone and hurt, and the knot began to pulse and grow like red coals in a dying fire after it's been stirred.

It was a little past midnight when Ted reached the Jeep. He shrugged off the backpack and unlocked the car door in one swift movement. With the help of the car's dome light he double checked the map so he wouldn't waste time getting lost. When he'd memorized the route to the closest city, Mill Hollow, he threw the unfolded map in the seat next to him and began down the mountain as fast as the night conditions allowed.

Chapter 7
Ryan – 12:49 a.m.

Ryan stopped to rest frequently. He sat against a tree and looked up at the full moon. He tried to ignore the gnawing of his stomach. It was over 24 hours since his last drink of water or bite of food. "There must be something I can eat." He began to run the possibilities over in his head. Wild animals were out of the question because he had no weapons, and even if he did somehow manage to kill a rabbit with a stone, he didn't have any matches to start a fire. *Who am I kidding anyway? I can't move that fast right now and I've never been a good pitcher. I couldn't hit a rabbit with a stone.* Ryan thought about Sneakers, the pet rabbit he and Ryan got when they were seven. Daydreaming about hitting Bugs Bunny with a stone almost made him laugh out loud. He wondered if he started laughing would he be able to stop?

He remembered seeing a movie about people in the wilderness eating the raw flesh of an animal and drinking its blood, *but that wasn't possible was it? What would I use to skin it? Animals were definitely off limits.* He'd been keeping his eye out for wild berries but it was either too early for some or too late for others because he hadn't seen any. Then he remembered a news story of an army pilot who'd kept himself alive by eating ants and grubs. *I've got to find something before it comes to that,* Ryan shuddered. To get the thought of eating bugs out of his mind, he began to name all the foods he'd eat when he was home with his family: "Pizza, Whoppers, Mom's spaghetti and meatballs, tacos, ice cold Coke, and peanut M&M's." This litany of foods made his mouth water. He swallowed, and continued on, "Peanut butter, Snickers, Chocolate Mint ice cream, chicken and rice...." His head hit his chest and Ryan slept uneasily, dreaming of his favorite foods.

Ted got to the sheriff's station in Mill Hollow by 2:30 a.m. *"About 20 hours!"* he fretted to himself as he looked at the digital readout of his watch. *"Ryan's been gone almost a whole day,"* he thought. The sheriff's office door was locked, but there was a light on and he could see a fat, dark haired man sleeping. His feet were on the desk and his hands were folded across an enormous belly. Ted figured this office served as emergency dispatch for ambulances as well as the lifeline for law around here. He banged on the window and the deputy's feet jerked to the floor. The deputy looked around, startled to see a stranger pounding on the glass. "Hold yer horses," he shouted angrily. "What can I do for ye?" he asked, yanking the door open with one hand and scratching his face with the other.

Relief flooded over Ted's exhausted body, like clouds providing temporary cover from the sun's heat. Finally, someone he could show his fear to, someone who could help get his son back. Ted walked through the door, relaying the story to the deputy in one long rush of words. The huge deputy made his way back behind the desk and opened one of the drawers. He produced a yellow legal pad and a pen. He looked at his watch and made a note on the paper, 2:37 a.m. Then he threw the pen down on the pad and propped his feet back up on the desk and put his hands behind his head.

31

Ted waited for some action. But after a few seconds of silence he shouted at the bovine deputy. "What are you doing? Every second counts. My son is missing! Didn't you hear me?"

"Yeah, I heard ye sir. I'm jist figgerin' who'd be best ta call ta head up the search party; Trapper Carr or Trapper Smith?"

"Get them both!" yelled Ted. I'll pay whatever it costs! Here, I brought my son's shirt for the dog's scent." Ted thrust a blue and grey checked flannel shirt across the table.

"Nope, no dogs. Dogs won't do no good."

"No dogs, why not?"

"Rain'll wash away the boy's scent."

Ted turned around looking first at the dry windows and then at this deputy whom he was beginning to worry was mentally deficient. "What rain?" Ted demanded.

"The rain that'll be here in 'bout an hour." Ted ignored that for a moment and asked for helicopters or search planes.

"Helicopters? Search planes?" laughed the deputy. "Where do ye think ye are? At the EFF – BEE – III? He exaggerated each letter for emphasis.

Ted tried to backtrack, realizing it wouldn't do any good to alienate this man. "I'm sorry," he said. "I'm upset, and new to this area. Please tell me what you *can* do to help me? My son's lost and alone. He's only thirteen years old." Ted's voice cracked and he coughed quickly to cover it up.

The deputy warmed a bit toward Ted. "Like I said," he drawled, "we's got two good trappers when it comes ta the part a the mountains ye was describin' ta me. Now

Trapper Carr, who I do believe is the right person for this job, lives 'bout thirty minutes from here. Trapper Smith is closer but one of his youngen's took sick yesterday and he probably won't want ta leave home."

Ted's patience was running thin again. He listened to the deputy's ramblings for another minute before interrupting him. "Call the Sheriff. I need someone with more authority! Get him on the phone right now. I can't afford to waste any more time with you. My son's life's in danger!"

The deputy looked angrily at Ted but he reached for the phone and punched in the Sheriff's home number. "Yeah Sheriff, it's me Earl. Sorry ta wake ye so early but I got kind of an emergency here."

Ted grabbed the phone away from him and began to tell the story again. Sheriff Martin was standing by the side of his bed dressed in striped pajama bottoms and a white tee shirt. He listened to Ted and motioned for his wife to go back to sleep. About halfway through the story he took his uniform out of the closet. "I'll be at the office in ten minutes sir, try and relax. And in the meantime Mr. Burns, why don't ye lie down on one of the bunks and get some rest. You'll need it when the rain stops." Ted hung up the phone and sat down, putting his head in his hands. He wondered what these people knew about the weather that he didn't.

Ryan – 3:08 a.m.

Ryan woke up disoriented. It was dark and he was lying on his left side. His body felt sore and stiff and he tried to get up but a sharp pain in his chest stopped him. *Why do I hurt so much? Why am I all wet? Where's my sleeping bag?*

33

Then with a rush, it came barreling back to him. He was lost and alone in the Appalachian Mountains. He'd fallen and hurt himself, and it was raining. "It's raining," he laughed, realizing this was the first good luck he'd had all day. He opened his mouth wide, more alert than he'd been in hours. He needed water and for now he could at least get his mouth wet. Soon, if it rained enough, he could drink water that would collect in low places. *I may be lost,* he reminded himself, *but I'm not going to die of thirst.* He laid back, closed his eyes, and cupped his hands around his mouth letting the sweet drops fall into his mouth.

Ben and his mom were in the tent listening to the steady beat of rain. It was a lonely sound, one that made the silence between them grow louder. Ben was in his dad's sleeping bag and occasionally dozed off until a clap of thunder or streak of lightning woke him. Then his heart would start to pound and with a sinking rush he remembered all over again that he was in his mom and dad's tent, not with Ryan - not with the one person in the world who understood everything about him. A feeling close to guilt, but one he couldn't quite name settled into the pit of his stomach.

His mom was sitting on top of her sleeping bag, rocking back and forth. She had her arms wrapped around her pillow and was shivering. Ben tried to make her get inside her bag but she refused. She couldn't stand the thought of being warm and safe when her son was cold and wet. She'd give anything to exchange places with him. Her mind had fixated on a single thought, which had become like a mantra to her, "Life as I know it will not go on until Ryan's back with me. Life as I know it will not go on until Ryan's back with me." Ben put one of his dad's shirts around his mom's shoulders but she shrugged it off and rocked back and forth. Ben had never felt so alone.

Mill Hollow – 4:49 a.m.

A crack of thunder, loud enough to jar Ted awake, was followed by a flash of lightning. It lit up the small cell he was in. *So here's the rain they've been talking about.* He looked at his watch; 4:49 a.m. He'd been asleep for two hours. He jumped up and looked out at the sheriff's office. Panic coursed through his veins like a sled slipping down an icy slope. *Two hours! How could I have slept two hours while Ryan's missing, or worse?* He saw Deputy 'Dumb' sitting with his feet propped up again, talking to another man in uniform. He dragged himself out of the cell and stretched his arms in front of him to ease some of the tension out of his back.

"Howdy," said the other uniformed man. He extended his hand toward Ted. "You look exhausted."

Ted stuck his hand out and pumped the sheriff's saying, "I'm Ted Burns.

"Glad ta meet ye, I'm John Martin," responded the sheriff, taking Ted's hand and gripping it. "We're gonna git yer boy back fer ye." Ted shook his head and went over to the window. He rested his hands on either side of the dark rectangle and stared into the early morning. The bleakness of the weather seeped inside him and he shook his head.

"Dogs are out of the question now aren't they?" he asked, already knowing the answer.

Sheriff Martin handed Ted a steaming cup of coffee. "Yes, I'm afraid they are Mr. Burns. Any trail yer son may've left'll be washed clean away. But we got word out ta the locals. They'll be gatherin' here at six, just about an hour from now." Ted glanced at the clock on the wall and shook his head. The sheriff continued, "We'll be led by the best scout in the area." The sheriff walked closer to Ted and laid his hand on his shoulder. "I've got a boy too. I know how ye feel."

"No you don't!" Ted shot back, angrily shrugging the sheriff's hand from his shoulder. "Your boy's safe at home in his own bed! And your wife's in a warm bed too! You didn't drag *your* family into the mountains to chase a boyhood fantasy about eagles! You can't possibly know how I feel." Ted finished the last words turning back to the window, trying to compose himself before tears popped into view. He laid his head against the cool glass of the window and stared at the downpour, wondering if Ryan had found a place to stay dry. The sheriff let his hand fall from Ted's shoulder and retreated to his desk, leaving the stranger alone.

Chapter 8
June 27

Six o'clock couldn't come fast enough for Ted. He checked his watch a hundred times and drank five cups of coffee while praying for enough people to be willing to get out of their beds and traipse over the mountains in the rain looking for a boy they didn't know.

About 6:10 the first two volunteers arrived, followed by a dozen others. Each offered their condolences or words of encouragement. Ted's heart filled with the goodness of these people and he began to believe Ryan would be found and everything could return to normal.

By 6:40 everyone had been briefed and 28 people were loaded into trucks heading to the mountains. Ted and the scout, Henry Carr, were in the lead. Mr. Carr tried talking but Ted wasn't interested and after a half an hour the trapper exhausted all he could think of to discuss with this man. They drove on in silence.

Camp – 7:00 a.m.

"I can't sit here anymore Ben! I need to do something! Where's Dad?"

"I don't know, but we have to stay here. What if Ryan comes back, or what if we got lost too?" Ben's voice cracked and he stopped trying to reason with his mom.

Sarah managed a smile for her son. "You're right honey. I'll go make us breakfast. How about pancakes now that the rain's stopped?"

Ben wasn't sure he could choke anything down, but making pancakes would give his mom something to do. "Yeah, pancakes sound great."

Ryan was shivering so violently that his teeth were chattering. His arms were wrapped around him and his clothes were soaked. He wondered if it was possible for skin to get waterlogged because he'd never felt so wet in all his life. He knew the little bit of rain he'd been able to collect in his mouth had not done his body much good. He felt weak and his head buzzed. He kept blinking to clear his eyes, but everything looked far away with indistinct edges. It had been a day and two nights since he'd last eaten and he thought of that last evening meal. His dad made freeze-dried chicken and rice and they'd eaten it around a campfire, with s'mores for dessert. Ryan thought nothing had ever tasted so good. After dinner his family played animal charades and laughed and talked until his parents went to bed. It seemed like an eternity ago and he'd give anything to be back, safe with them. *I won't get there feeling sorry for myself,* he thought.

Ryan got up, feeling like he'd been used for a punching bag. He tried to wipe away some of the mud that had spattered on him. The energy it took wasn't worth it and he gave up. The sun was beginning to warm the ground and mist formed in a few places as the rain evaporated. *Evaporation,* he thought. *I need to find water before it's all gone!* He clutched his walking stick and started off in search of a place where the rain collected overnight. His slow movements reminded him of a sloth and he let out a gruff snort at the sight of himself covered with green moss. He favored his left side, which hurt more than his right, but even moving at this pace the pain was almost unbearable. He switched the walking stick from hand to hand often keeping his eyes open for water sitting in the depressions of rocks or logs.

Twenty minutes later he found an inviting puddle in the middle of a pile of rocks. He sank down on his knees paying no attention to the cut on his leg, which opened again. He let the walking stick fall beside him, cupped his hands in the cool water and drank greedily. He couldn't get it up to his mouth fast enough so he plunged his face into the water and drank. He drank until he felt full and then rinsed his hands and face, leaving the puddle blood tinged. He sat back and stretched out his legs, lying against a tree.

It felt good to have his stomach full. He settled further against the tree and let the sun start to dry his clothes. He felt hopeful again, like maybe he would be okay and his family would find him today. Then the cups of water Ryan drank began to rumble and gurgle. He started to feel queasy and began to sweat. The water rushed back up his throat and forced him to lurch over and heave back into the small pool, and with it went all his newfound hope.

Ben bent over, picked up a small stone and threw it against a tree. His actions were automatic; no thought was needed. His mom stared into the fire, which was all she'd done since making pancakes. She was acting weird, like this was happening to *her*, instead of the whole family. Ben felt sorry for himself, *If anybody has a right to feel bad it should be me. I'm the one who lost a twin, a part of me. She doesn't even know I'm here.* He shook his head to clear it of negative thoughts, and stopped tossing pebbles to look at his mom. She was staring into her coffee cup. Seeing his mom like this angered Ben, and he wanted to scream at her. Instead he went back to throwing rocks, a little more forcefully.

Sarah worried that her husband had gotten lost or run off the road last night, or worse. Every time she emptied her head the thoughts crept back in. She knew she had enough real things going on without making up scenarios about what might have happened to Ted, but her mind was only thinking of doom and gloom. She glanced over at her son. *What's wrong with me? I should be over there with Ben trying to comfort him. I'm supposed to be the mom, not a basket case.* She set her coffee down and scrunched her face between her hands. *It's been too long. Ryan's got to be hurt, or worse. Has he found anything to eat? God please help my boy! Please help my boy!*

Sarah picked her coffee up and morbid thoughts persisted. She felt like she was in the middle of a nightmare. The latest plot was one in which her son was mauled by a bear, just yards away from her tent. She could hear his screams, but she couldn't find him. She kept having this nightmare, or something similar, in broad daylight, huddled over a cold cup of coffee, totally ignoring her other son. She wasn't sure how much longer she could wait here doing nothing. She felt useless and angry, and each time one of Ben's rocks hit a tree it made an annoying pinging sound making her even angrier. Sarah wanted to shout at Ben, to make him stop the noise; she barely kept it in check.

She knew it wasn't Ben's fault that Ryan was gone, even though she kept asking herself why he hadn't woken up when Ryan left? She was lost in these angry thoughts when Ben came running over to her. He was saying something but she couldn't make it out. Ben started shaking his mom's arm. She just wanted to be left alone inside her own head. "Mom! Mom! Dad's coming. Can you hear him?" Something pierced her consciousness and she shot up, nearly stumbling into the fire, turning to meet the shouts.

"Ben! Sarah!"

"We're here Dad," cried Ben. He was supporting his mom who had dropped the tin cup of coffee at her feet. She broke free of Ben and ran toward the sound of her husband's voice. The hurt on Ben's face went unnoticed by Sarah. Despite his rumpled clothes and several days' growth of beard, her husband had never looked so good to her. Sarah ran to him but Ted kept walking with her until he reached Ben and could hug them both. Their faces told him all he needed to know without asking; they were both physically okay, and Ryan had not come back.

The guide and the volunteers stood back waiting for the reunion to end. Sarah pushed herself away from Ted, realizing there were people staring at her. "Are these people here to find Ryan?" she asked Ted. Heads nodded in the crowd and people began talking quietly. Sheriff Martin and Henry Carr stepped forward to introduce themselves to Sarah. The sheriff stayed to talk with Sarah while Henry began to organize the volunteers.

"Leon, grab six people and head over..."

"Where are the dogs?" interrupted Sarah frantically.

Sorry Ma'am, dogs aint no good after a hard rain like we had last night," answered the trapper.

"Then you've got planes out searching?" Her head whipped around looking at the cloudless sky. The sheriff shook his head and Ted reached for his wife. He pulled her head to focus on his face and tried to explain what had already been explained to him hours earlier. She brushed away his hands and shouted, "No planes either!"

This time it was Trapper Carr who looked to Ted for help and then said quickly, "We're wastin' time here Mr. Burns, kin ye take yer wife somewheres else ta explain thin's to her?" Ted shook his head, fully understanding his wife's bewilderment. He took a firm hold of her by the shoulder and turned her toward their tent.

Trapper Carr began his instructions again to the volunteers. Ben took all this in unnoticed by his parents and strangers alike. Then he approached the trapper and said, "Excuse me sir, I'd like to help too."

"Ye kin best help us son by stayin' here with yer Ma and makin' sure she's okay. Losin' a loved one kin git ye tetched in the haid," he said tapping his head.

"But I really can help. Ryan's not just my brother. We're identical twins." A low rumble of voices ran through the crowd. Ben heard it and spoke loudly enough for everyone to hear him. "Ryan looks just like me, so take a good look." He paused for a few seconds and then continued. "Because we're identical twins I can feel things about Ryan. I may be able to sense if we're going in the right direction. So which group should I be with?" He was once again looking directly at Trapper Carr.

Mr. and Mrs. Burns came out of their tent and heard what Ben was saying. His dad put his arm around his son's shoulders and spoke firmly. "Ben your place is with your mother at camp."

Ben's face fell and he jerked an angry look at his mom, a look that cut through Sarah's self-pity. She knew if she couldn't get herself together and let Ben go with the search party, she'd lose him, as surely as she'd lost Ryan. "Go," she said to him. "I'll be fine back here in case Ryan comes. Go and find him Ben!" Sarah's voice cracked as she said this and then she turned away from the crowd.

The search parties spread out. Each group had a leader, compasses, several backpacks containing food, water, space blankets, and first aid kits, as well as walkie-talkies, and flares to shoot when Ryan was found. They were to search all morning and into dusk if necessary, then return to camp, but there was a general feeling that they'd bring the boy back before then.

Ryan – 2:00 p.m.

The sun was blindingly bright, adding to Ryan's weak and dizzy feelings. He had welcomed the warmth of it when it was drying his clothes, but now it was just another annoyance. His eyes grew foggier and he began to see sun-rings around things. He knew something was wrong with his body, something other than the cuts and bruises, and his rib hurting, something other than being hungry and thirsty. He could feel himself slipping away, and a part of him welcomed it. But another part, a part deep in his soul, something primal, was still trying to survive. It told him that everything really wasn't moving and that trees didn't have halos around them. This part of him was fading. His eyes were dry and scratchy, his ears were buzzing, and numbness was creeping into his limbs. With every passing minute the hallucinations seemed more and more real.

At first he thought he saw Ben sitting under a tree, but when he got there it had only been a shrub. Then he saw the tents, but soon realized they were rocks. At one point he was sure he smelled pancakes, but couldn't manage to follow the smell. He had a continual gnawing in his stomach. The ringing in his ears was so loud that he thought someone was talking to him in a foreign language. If he could just make out what they were saying he might be able to find his way back to his family. His tongue was swollen. He kept biting it and tasting blood in his mouth. Phantom voices outside his head, began to call to him. He told himself they weren't real, but they persisted. Then he began to think maybe they were real voices so he listened for a while and then shouted out, turning around in a circle. The twirling made Ryan dizzy. He fell to the ground in a heap of hurt and bewilderment. *"Sleep,"* he thought, *"I'll just sleep here for a few minutes and then I'll feel better. Ben will find me if I just stay here and sleep."*

Chapter 10
Amos – 3:32 p.m.

Amos Riley was a big man, at least six-foot-four. His stringy black hair and beard were both streaked with grey. His hair hung a foot beneath the battered leather hat on his head. He wore a deerskin jacket, jeans and boots. His horse, Nearly, named because she was *nearly* as good as his last horse, was a dapple grey who stood seventeen hands at her shoulders. "A big horse, for a big man," Ma liked to say.

Amos was out wandering the hills, checking traps and keeping his eyes open for rabbit and squirrel. His shotgun was stuck in his saddle. Nearly was used to the hills and was as sure footed as mountain horses came. So when she let out a whinny and her forelocks trembled Amos paid attention. Her nostrils worked the mountain air, and she held her head high.

"What ye smellin' Nearly?" asked Amos petting his horse. "Do ye smell us some supper?" He kept a light rein on Nearly and let her choose the trail while he surveyed the trees. "There ain't no supper here 'bouts girl." But Nearly answered him with another whinny. Amos looked around again, this time letting his eyes search the ground for a snake, sometimes they made Nearly nervous. Then he saw it, a crumpled heap at the base of a tree, about 20 yards off to his left. He drew out his shotgun and dismounted. Nearly stayed put, happy to nibble at patches of grass. Amos approached the form on the ground cautiously. His gun was cocked. When he reached the body he called out, "Hey, what's wrong with ye? Is ye hairt?" Amos took the last few steps realizing that the body was that of a boy and his heart beat faster. He turned the boy over using the tip of his gun. Ryan now lay flat on his back. His head lolled to one side and his eyes closed. The mountain man clicked the safety back on his gun and set it down before he dropped to one knee. His heart leapt in his chest as he got a closer look at the child. "Charlie! Charlie!" he cried out. "Ye've come back ta us. Wait 'til yer ma sees ye!" Amos picked up Ryan as if he were a feather pillow and carried him back to Nearly. He laid him carefully on the ground and began to check him over. His fingers probed Ryan's legs, arms, belly, and back, searching for an injury that would make the boy sick. Satisfied there was nothing of consequence, he lifted a water bag from his horse and held it to Ryan's lips. The water trickled into Ryan's mouth and revived him just enough so that he grabbed at the bag with both hands and pulled it to him. His eyes were still closed, but he drank thirstily. "No, Charlie, that's enough fer now. I'll git ye ta yer ma. She'll know what ta do."

Ryan was only vaguely aware of words being said to him. He drifted off again as the mountain man laid him across Nearly's saddle. Amos retrieved his gun and began to guide his horse back home. Amos had known his son would come back to him. He knew Charlie hadn't really died in that horrible accident. It had all been a mistake and now his mind was filled with thoughts of how happy Ma'd be when she saw their boy again. He could hardly wait to get home, but he didn't hurry. He had his precious son back and he wouldn't let anything happen to him ever again.

Camp – 6:30 p.m.

Sarah kept herself busy scanning the horizon for a flare. It would mean they'd found Ryan. She wouldn't know in what condition, but they would have found him and for now that was all that mattered. Hours passed. Her eyes grew strained from watching. Her nerves stretched tighter and tighter. She rubbed at the crick in her neck and imagined several times she'd seen a flare, but it was only wishful thinking. The sky stayed as empty as her heart.

Chapter 11
Amos – 7:21 p.m.

"Ma! Ma!" Amos stopped Nearly in front of a small log house. The roof was made of rusted tin and there were two square windows on either side of the beat-up wooden door. Faded blue calico curtains hung in both windows. "Ma! Git out here. Charlie needs yer help!" Amos gently lifted Ryan down from Nearly and walked toward the house. Ma, Lizzie Sue, came rushing out. She was a small woman, barely five feet tall and no more than 100 pounds. She had frizzy red hair tied at her neck, but curls escaped everywhere around her face. She wore a long denim skirt, hiking boots and a dark blouse. A calico apron made of the same material as the window curtains, was tied around her waist. Lizzie Sue held one side of the apron tightly in her left hand. Her right hand was clenched at her mouth, biting a knuckle.

All the color drained from Lizzie Sue's face as she saw Amos carrying a boy with dark curly hair like Charlie's. At the thought of her dead son she turned to the cross on the hill about 30 yards from their house. The cross-marked the grave of her boy, dead now for a year. "It's Charlie, Ma. I know'd he'd come back! He jist got lost and hungry and needs yer help. I got ta git him ta his bed."

Lizzie tore her eyes away from the cross on the hill and concentrated on her husband's face. Amos was flushed with excitement. His eyes had that crazed look she'd seen so often since Charlie died. He wasn't making any sense, but she followed him into the house without a word. Lizzie Sue grabbed the candle off the kitchen table and climbed the six rungs of the ladder to the loft where a straw mattress was rolled up in the corner. As small as she was, she could barely stand in the loft. She unrolled the mattress, pounding out the worst of the lumps. Next she took a handmade quilt from a peg in the corner and shook it once over the wooden railing. Dust motes floated onto the kitchen and sitting room below.

Amos waited patiently on the second rung, holding Ryan in his arms. "Git out the way now Lizzie and I'll lay 'im down." Lizzie Sue stood off to the side and watched Amos lay the boy on the old mattress, which had once belonged to Charlie.

Lizzie Sue had long ago gotten used to the size of her husband. He was over a foot taller than her and weighed more than double. She looked out for her feet when Amos was around. Once the boy was on the mattress Lizzie Sue started examining him. She began with his eyes, lifting first the right eyelid and then the left. The black part in the middle of the boy's eyes was bigger than it should be. She felt his forehead and it was hot and clammy. She ran her finger over the cut above his eye. Next she probed his swollen tongue and smelled his shallow breath. She laid her head on his chest to better hear his heart. Ryan moaned softly rasping, "Mom? Mom?"

Lizzie Sue's own breath caught in her chest. "He knows yer touch Ma," said Amos who had been watching his wife. Lizzie Sue bit her lower lip, a habit she had when she was nervous. Next she prodded the boy's ribs and he cried out. She thoroughly checked his limbs and noted the gash on his knee. It was swollen, hot, and crusted with dirt. It would have to be cleaned and stitched. Once she was done checking

the boy over Lizzie Sue bounced to her feet, and shooed Pa
off the ladder so she could get to her medicine bag.
The few people who lived on the mountain knew
Lizzie Sue as a natural healer. She took a teakettle off the
stove and brought it to the pump at the sink. She primed the
pump twice and held the kettle under the cool mountain
water. After stoking the fire in the cast iron stove she put the
kettle on one of the burners. Next she took an old brown
leather suitcase from under the sink and hefted it to the pine
table in the middle of the floor and opened it flat.
Amos watched her from his rocker by the fireplace.
He lit his pipe and chewed on the end of it. He knew ma
would make Charlie better so he left her alone with her
doctoring things. Lizzie Sue chose a small paper bag of dried
leaves and sprinkled some in a cup. Replacing that bag, she
opened another with dried flowers and crushed one of the
smaller buds into the same cup.
Stacked on pine shelves were ironed pieces of an old
sheet. She chose a piece and began to tear it into strips. She
heard the boy calling out for his ma and both she and Amos
glanced at the loft. "Good ta hear noise agin ain't it Lizzie?
Charlie's come home Ma."
"Hmmph," was all she answered as she walked to the
kettle and poured boiling water over the crushed leaves and
flowers. She left the cup of herbs on the table to steep and
filled a bowl with more hot water. After placing strips of
cloth in the water she rubbed a bar of handmade soap around
in the bowl, ignoring the heat of the water. She crossed the
few feet to where Pa was sitting and handed him the bowl.
Lizzie Sue climbed the loft ladder and held out her hands for
Amos to give her the bowl. She knelt next to Ryan and began

to unbutton his shirt, noticing again how much he resembled Charlie; same hair, same nose, about the same size and age. She loosened the laces on his shoes and took them off along with his torn and filthy jeans, and then set about cleaning Ryan's cuts. She rubbed carefully at first and rinsed the cloth often, thankful that the moaning boy couldn't fully feel what she was doing.

When the water was bright red with Ryan's blood she handed the bowl to Amos and made her way back to the kitchen to get clean water. On the third trip she stopped at her sewing basket and plucked out a needle and thread.

Lizzie threaded the needle with a long piece of black thread. The cut above Ryan's eye took eight small stitches, but the gash by his knee required more than twice as many. The boy moaned each time she took a stitch and it pained her as much as it did him. Several times Lizzie Sue thought about stopping, but knew she had to see it through to the end or the boy wouldn't heal properly. He looked so much like her boy she wanted to leave as small a scar as possible. When she was finished she sat back on her haunches and asked Pa to get her the rest of the white cloths. She tore these into long strips, each about three inches wide. With pa's help she wrapped the strips around Ryan's chest, head and leg. Satisfied with her work she asked Amos to hand up the tea. Amos was always a little in awe of Ma's doctoring ability.

Lizzie Sue dipped the last piece of cloth in the tea. She held it to Ryan's lips and squeezed a few drops at a time down his throat. She didn't know what the boy had eaten lately but by the look of his swollen tongue she knew he needed liquids. She wanted the herbs to work slowly so she patiently repeated the wetting and squeezing until the tea was almost gone. Then she got up to make a mustard poultice for the boy's chest, and steep some willow bark to help ease his pain and fever.

Chapter 12
Camp – 9:07 p.m.

The volunteers searched for Ryan until dusk. They stopped only to drink from canteens or eat an energy bar. They straggled back to camp in small groups, each one shaking their heads and shrugging their shoulders. Even though she'd seen no flare, Sarah still searched every returning party for a glimmer of hope. The volunteers had seen this before. Sometimes they were lucky and brought back a loved one, other times they'd been able to bring back a body to be buried, which helped give closure to the family. Even that was preferable to days like today. Times like this were the worst, no body, no word, no trace, just anguish, questions and grief to deal with.

Ted and Ben's team were the last to make it back. Ben felt awkward facing his mom, like he let her down, like he'd let everyone down. He'd been so sure he could lead them to Ryan, so sure he could feel his way to his twin once he was further out in the mountains. But it hadn't happened yesterday and it hadn't happened today. What good were these twin connections if they didn't work when you needed them most?

At about three-thirty this afternoon Ben *had* sensed a flurry of movement around Ryan. He'd stopped walking to let the feelings wash over him. He sensed someone around his twin, but it was a weak link and the moment passed as quickly as it had come. Ben started walking again and hadn't said anything about it. After all, what could he say? But then he'd had similar twinges a few hours later. This time the feelings had a variety of activity connected with them, especially near Ryan's head and leg. After that he felt nothing, no matter how hard he concentrated.

Ben decided not to tell his mom about the feelings, but when he saw her puffy eyes and swollen face he changed his mind. She looked scared and was carrying Ryan's vest like it was a life preserver thrown to her in deep water. He had to give her something else to hang onto, something other than Ryan's vest. So the first chance he got he pulled her into the tent and discussed the day with her.

"This happened twice? This feeling of hands on Ryan?" Sarah was trying to make sense of Ben's story.

"Yes," Ben was shaking his head, "and then a while after that I felt more peaceful and I think Ryan did too." He hadn't meant to embellish his story, but he couldn't take it back now.

"You're certain of that? More peaceful? What do you think that means? I think it's good don't you?"

"Sure Mom, peaceful, not scared, it's a good feeling." Ben was in over his head and was sorry he'd decided to tell her anything.

"Peaceful," repeated his mom. Ben just looked at her. "Not a dead kind of peaceful though, right?" Her voice was verging on hysteria and Ben was getting creeped out.

"No," he shouted, "not dead…just peaceful!"

"Okay, okay," she said looking around the tent. The look in her eyes scared Ben and he wondered when the last time was that his mom had slept or eaten. "I think it means someone is helping him, Ben! Someone is taking care of Ryan. Don't you see he'll be okay? We'll get him back."

"Mom," started Ben, but his mom interrupted him and moved ahead with her own thoughts.

"It's got to mean he's alive, he's safe somewhere and we just need to find that place where he's safe. Don't let anyone tell you differently! I don't care how long it takes!" Sarah's voice was high and thin and Ben thought he should get his dad, but his mom grabbed his shoulders and looked him in the face. "Do you hear me? I don't care how long it takes. We're a team. It doesn't matter what those people out there think. Ryan's alive! Tears were streaming down her cheeks and she was shaking Ben back and forth, shouting, "Tell me you feel him! Tell me you feel him!"

Sarah's hysterical cries brought Ted to the door of the tent. "Sarah!" he said more sternly than he'd meant, "the volunteers are leaving. Get hold of yourself!" Sarah whipped her head around and searched the face of her husband for some hint of compassion, or love, and found none. She hadn't loosened her grip on Ben and her eyes shot back to her son.

"Ben, come outside and thank the search parties. Leave your mother here." Ben shook off his mother's grip and moved toward his dad. Sarah let her hands fall to her sides and hung her head. Ted held the tent flap open for his son and stepped aside. Ben's feelings were tripping all over each other. He thought he might explode or cry, or hit someone, or all three, he wasn't sure. Instead, he obediently followed his dad.

Sarah went outside too and Ben looked back at his mom before going further and said, "I believe too, Mom."

Sarah didn't acknowledge with words what Ben said, but a smile crossed her face and she hugged Ryan's survival vest. Ben and Ted returned to the tent about ten minutes later to find Sarah curled up in a ball, still hanging onto Ryan's vest. "We need to talk Sarah," said Ted gently. She rolled over on her back and stared into the blackness of the tent. "Ben would you start a fire while your mother and I talk. We'll need to get dinner soon."

Ben turned to leave when he heard his mom say, "Anything you want to say to me, you can say in front of Ben. We're a team!"

"No, Sarah, we're a team," shouted Ted, pointing to himself and his wife. "Ben's our son and not everything I say needs to be heard by him." He turned to face Ben. "Get the fire going, we'll be out in a few minutes." Ben left. He knew nobody felt like eating but he didn't want to stay and listen to his parents argue either.

"Sarah, the searchers aren't coming back tomorrow."

"Why not? Surely they haven't given up already!"

Ted hung his head and answered, "Before they left, the sheriff pulled me aside and told me the volunteers covered more area today in any direction than Ryan could possibly have traveled on foot."

"Well he just didn't drop off the face of the earth, Ted!"

Ted was tired and hurting. He had no more patience for his wife. They needed to be strong for Ben. "As a matter of fact Sarah, that's probably exactly what happened! Mr. Carr thinks Ryan was dragged or fell over a cliff…"

"Then search the ravines!" she shouted.

"Do you know how many ravines there are, and how many we've already searched? And that's probably not all that happened to him." Ted's voice broke and he looked away from Sarah wondering if he should go into the details the trapper had given him.

"Tell me Ted. Tell me what you're thinking and then I'll tell you what I *know!*" Ted let out a sigh and covered his face with his hands. Only the shaking of his shoulders gave away the tears he was shedding. "Tell me Ted. Get it all out in the open!"

Ted dropped his hands and turned to face his wife. "Sarah what do you suppose happens to a body in the mountains? There's bears, mountain lions and vultures for starters." Sarah took all of this in without blinking and then she took her husband's tear soaked hands in hers.

"None of that has anything to do with our son. Do you hear me Ted? He's okay. He's not down in some ravine. He's okay. I know it in here." She pointed to her heart. "And I know it in here." She tapped her head.

"You're living in a fairy tale Sarah! They found blood and part of Ryan's shirt. They found mountain lion tracks. You put it together."

"It's not Ryan's blood, I know it, and so does that boy out by the fire." Sarah jerked her head towards Ben outside the tent. We're not giving up. You've got five days left of your vacation and Ben and I have two months before school starts. We'll find him Ted." He pulled his hand away from Sarah's grip, but she continued, "You're either with us or you're against us. What's it going to be?"

"Don't turn this into a you against me game." Ted's angry voice carried out to Ben who put his hands over his ears to block out the argument.

"The Sheriff took a blood sample from Ben and will have it analyzed along with some of the blood from the ground. He'll have the results in a few days and he'll let us know if it was Ryan's blood by the tracks." Ted turned away from his wife to go to his son. Sarah hugged Ryan's vest and started humming a mindless tune.

Dinner was quiet and tense. The freeze-dried chili and crackers were hard for Ben to swallow sitting across from his silent parents. To keep himself from throwing the chili into the fire, or jumping up and shouting at them he concentrated on trying to make a connection to Ryan. Nothing materialized; there was a black void, and this scared him more than how his parents were acting. His thoughts started running in too many directions; he wondered if Ryan had anything to eat, if he was hurt, where he was, what was happening to his mom and dad? Then he wondered if his parents blamed him for Ryan going off alone, and for not being able to connect with him? The awful thought that made Ben throw the rest of his chili into the fire and stalk off to his tent, was, *Do they wish it were me instead of Ryan?*

As soon as Ben entered his tent he froze. He'd never spent a night alone. Even before he was born Ryan was with him, and last night he'd been with his mom. But there was no one tonight. His heart hammered and his head pounded. He thought about asking to sleep with his parents but knew they wouldn't fill the emptiness. He laid down in his brother's sleeping bag and smelled the scent of him. He squeezed his eyes shut and opened himself up to any feelings that might come. Slowly his mind relaxed and he filled with a sense of peace mixed with something else. *What is it? Fear? No. Anger? No. Confusion? Maybe. I know you're still out there Ryan. Can you hear me? Hang in there, we'll get you back and everything will be okay again.* Ben whispered this silent prayer again and again until he fell into an exhausted sleep.

   When Sheriff Martin and Ted Burns met at the designated spot three days later all that was delivered was bad news. The blood they had taken from Ben matched the blood found by the mountain lion tracks. All other inquiries the Sheriff put out amounted to nothing. No one had seen the boy, and locals thought no one ever would. The most likely scenario, given the blood, the lion tracks and the piece of shirt was that Ryan had been attacked by a mountain lion and dragged off.

   There were lots of unanswered questions, but Sheriff Martin had seen stranger things. The hardest part now would be getting the family to believe it.

PART TWO
- FEAR -

Chapter 13
July 2

Six days later Ryan woke feeling better. He was more clear-headed than he'd been in a while. The swelling in his tongue was gone. He was able to keep food and water down that the lady with the red hair brought him three times each day. It didn't hurt so much when he took a deep breath either. His nightmares were gone and he knew he'd be reunited with his family soon. He was grateful to the people who were caring for him, especially the woman, but he didn't quite understand where he was and who these people were, and most importantly he wondered why the man kept calling him Charlie?

Even when he was at his weakest he tried to tell these people his real name. The man, who was scary just to look at, gruffly told him not to say that anymore, and the woman told him that if he knew what was good for him he'd keep still about what his name was. There was something about the way she said it that made Ryan not ask too many more questions while he was still weak. Each night before he went to sleep he vowed that when he was feeling strong enough to get up, he'd thank them for saving his life, and then demand to be taken to his parents. He might even offer them a reward and from the look of this house they could use the money.

Ryan wasn't sure how long he'd been here, wherever here was, in this tiny house lying on this lumpy mattress. Last night when the woman took the cloth bandages from his head, chest and leg, to wash his wounds and put on some fresh leafy things, Ryan tried to get her to talk to him. She didn't say much, but what she did say worried him. She told him to watch himself around Amos, and not to cross him if he knew what was good for him. After she left him for the night he laid awake poking at the uncomfortable mattress, trying to put everything together. He remembered following the eagle, getting lost, and falling down the hill. He remembered something about a mountain lion and spending the night alone, but the rest was a blur to him. The woman hadn't put the bandages back on last night, which Ryan took as a good sign, and now his hands absently explored the stitches above his eye and by his knee. He wondered what his face looked like but there wasn't even a window to catch his reflection in, much less a mirror. *Well, at least people won't have any trouble telling Ben and me apart anymore.* His heart skipped a beat as Ben came to mind; something, which happened a hundred times a day now that he was awake for long periods of time. He missed his twin more than he missed his mom and dad. *Mom and dad are going to be so mad when I get home.*

As these thoughts occupied Ryan's mind, Lizzie Sue climbed the ladder to check on him. She didn't say anything when she found Ryan awake. She began her morning routine, starting with pulling at his eyelids to study his eyes. Next she looked at how the stitches had fared during the night without being covered, and finally listened to his breathing. Then she gave him the glass jar to use and turned to leave. "Wait!" Ryan said more forcefully than he meant. "I mean *please* wait." Lizzie turned around on the ladder and looked at Ryan. He smiled and said, "I don't need this anymore," and pointed to the jar. "I can make it to the bathroom on my own now."

Lizzie Sue looked at him and said, "Ye need more healin' time," and turned around to start down the ladder.

"You've been saying that to me every day, but I really am feeling better.' This declaration didn't stop Lizzie Sue. She proceeded down the few steps of the ladder and Ryan heard her move to the kitchen. *How long have I been here?* he wondered. It was time for some answers. He felt clear-headed and he sure as heck wanted to get off this pokey mattress. *What was in it anyway?* He got to his knees, judging that he'd have to be careful standing in the small loft. He reached for the clothes next to him and put on a shirt first and then pants. He was surprised to learn how much this small effort tired him. Next he reached for his boots. It hurt to stretch and now that he was moving around a bit he felt dizzy and sweaty, but still determined to get up and face these people. He sat back and started lacing up one of his boots. He began to wonder about the clothes. They fit reasonably well; they just weren't his. There were no holes in the jeans and the waist was too big. The flannel shirt was mainly red where his had been mainly blue. He knew they couldn't be Amos' clothes and that was when he was startled by the enormous head and booming voice of the man who kept calling him Charlie.

"Ye're up Charlie! Did yer ma say twas okay? She may be little but she's fierce as a hungry bobcat when ye don't mind her!"

"I'm fine. I wanted to come and talk to you."

"Ye sound so strange Charlie. It's a wonder I kin make out what ye're sayin'." Amos backed down the ladder, making room for Ryan. Ryan made his way down the ladder. He didn't feel as strong as he thought he did and at the bottom he was happy to have floor beneath him. He felt light-headed and must have swayed a bit because Amos grabbed his shoulders and held onto him. Ryan looked around at the meager surroundings. There was a stone fireplace under the loft and two rocking chairs in front of it. One chair was small and the other was large. Ryan thought immediately of Goldilocks and the Three Bears. *All they need is a medium-sized chair and they'd be all set.* No sooner had he thought this strange thing than he saw a medium sized rocker in a corner. An oval rug lay on the pine floor between the chairs and the fireplace. Beside one chair was a sewing basket and beside the other chair was a block of wood with a knife stuck in it. Ryan could just make out the head of a bear emerging from the wood. A small plank table was set up behind the rockers. Directly behind the table was an old fashioned stove, and a sink with a pump coming out of it. The stove was like the ones at the downtown kid's museum that he and Ben used to visit. Completing the small house was another room with a curtain hanging in the doorway. Ryan couldn't see what was in it, but he assumed it was Amos and Lizzie Sue's bedroom.

"How are ye feelin' now Charlie?" asked Amos as he let go of Ryan's shoulders.

Ryan ignored the name for now and asked, "Where's the bathroom?" Ryan had been embarrassed when using the jar and the can the woman brought to the loft but there was no need for that anymore.

"The what?" laughed Amos. "Ye musta lost yer haid boy!"

Before Ryan could reply Lizzie Sue came in from outside carrying fresh eggs in her apron. She took in the scene and sat the eggs in a bowl in the sink. "Kin ye believe it Ma? Charlie fergot where the outhouse is. He musta bin out in that sun longer'n I thought." Amos was shaking his head and still chuckling. "Come here boy," said Lizzie Sue. She was holding the door open. Ryan went to her. "It's over there," she pointed to a small, weathered wooden box, no bigger than the broom closet at home.

Amos yelled out, laughing, "Don't spect no fancy paper neither." Ryan gingerly stepped outside into the warm mountain air. It felt glorious to him and he took a moment to look at his surroundings. Things were small and run down, but it was peaceful and smelled so clean. He wanted to show it to his family. *I'll be back with them soon,* he smiled.

Inside the house Lizzie Sue was saying, "Amos, be easy on the boy. He's unsure of his self in the mountains."

"Lizzie Sue have you gone soft in the haid too? Charlie knows these woods near good as I do. I should know, I taught him myself."

Lizzie Sue shook her head and watched the boy's retreating figure. She noted the dark curls and the set of his shoulders. Even walking away he looked like Charlie. Amos was happier and clearer-headed than he'd been since the accident. *Maybe if I just try a little harder I could believe this youngen' was our son too. Who'd be harmed? The boy'd be dead anyways if not fer Amos and me. Dead.* Her mind drifted to that night, almost a year ago, even though it seemed more like ten years. She'd played that day over and over again in her head.

Pa and Charlie had jist gone huntin' fer some stew meat. Charlie was only twelve then but Amos was sure he was ready ta go off huntin' by his self. He knew the mountains all right, thought Lizzie Sue. *And he knew the woods, but he didn't have a man's way a' huntin' bout him yet. He was always pullin' jokes on Pa, which is probably why he thought it'd be funny ta sneak up behind Pa and scare him. Amos'd been so intent on a deer he'd had in his sights so's when Charlie sprung up out of nowhere howlin' like a wolf Amos turned and shot him! And jist like that our life changed forever. Amos picked up Charlie and run with him back ta the house, leavin' Nearly ta fend fer herself. But it was no use. The bloody hole was jist too big for his small chest and nothin' in my doctorin' bag could save my boy.* She lost her only child who'd lived beyond the first months of birthing. Along with Charlie's death she also lost Amos, or at least the best part of him, until he'd found 'Charlie' again.

Lizzie Sue smiled to herself as she remembered checking the boy's stitches yesterday. They were ready to come out. Maybe today. He was a good boy, just like Charlie. *'This time it looks like I saved them both. The boy's lookin' good and Amos is laughin' agin. So why can't I jist make myself act like this boy is Charlie come back ta us?'*

Chapter 14
July 7

Ted's heart grew harder with each passing day that he and Ben returned empty handed to the tent. In his mind, he knew there was no chance Ryan would be found alive. In his heart he was sure he didn't want to bring back what was left of his son's body to his wife. They searched ravines and cliffs until one ravine began to look like every other, and still there had been no further clue of Ryan. Three more storms since Ryan had gone missing erased any chance they had for finding new traces of him.

Ben got quieter each day. Heaviness settled around him and anyone bothering to look at him would have called him depressed. He still got phantom twinges of Ryan at times but he didn't bother to tell his dad, and his dad had quit asking about them long ago. He saved these scraps of hope for his mom.

At dusk each day Ted and his son came back to the tent to face a 'cheerleader' Sarah. That was how Ted had begun to think of her - Sarah, a cheerleader for the 'Ted and Ben Team'. A team she was counting on to bring back the trophy, a prize more cherished than her own life. Sarah was so sure of Ryan's return that she was no longer discouraged by her husband's sour moods. She looked forward to the time she and Ben shared after dinner each night. While Ted updated the log of their daily movements, Ben and his mom sat by the fire and he told her about connections he'd felt to Ryan that day. It didn't matter how many times Sarah heard the same thing, she listened intently, and always ended the conversation with the same question to Ben, "You still believe he'll come back, don't you Ben?"

And just before Ben threw dirt on the fire to put it out for the night he responded, "Sure we'll find him Mom and everything will be just like it was before." Each night Ben trudged to his tent, hating to enter the lifeless void. Everything around him felt cold and meaningless.

July 14

The days dragged on endlessly and now it was time for Ted to go back to work. His vacation days, and an extension he'd gotten from his partners, were used up. The real world was waiting and his boss deemed Ted had spent enough time searching the mountains. He wanted to bring his family back home with him, but no amount of pleading and reasoning would persuade Sarah to leave. Against his better judgment, Ted went to Mill Hollow and brought in provisions for Ben and Sarah. He trekked back to the campsite with a heavy heart that demonstrated itself in the slowness of his feet.

"Don't look so glum Ted you'll come see us on weekends." The 'cheerleader' was trying to motivate the team.

"Sarah, are we agreed that no matter what, you'll come back with me in two weeks? That will give you and Ben a good part of the summer to pull things together at home." Sarah knew that 'by pulling things together,' Ted meant getting on with life with only one son. She agreed to anything as long as she and Ben could stay on the mountain.

"Yes, Ted, we've been through all of this before. Ben and I'll leave in a few weeks, no matter what." Ted let the 'few weeks' remark go without emphasizing it was two weeks. Sarah continued, "But there'll be three of us going home with you." Her last words went several octaves higher and trilled off like a retreating siren.

Ted kissed his wife's forehead and turned to face Ben. "Come take a walk with me Ben." He fell in step with his Dad while Sarah put away the provisions. She was humming *Whistle While You Work*, the song from <u>Snow White</u>. "I don't have to tell you how worried I am about you and your Mom. I have no way of checking to see if you're okay. Cell phones don't work up here and I'm going to be hundreds of miles away."

"I know Dad."

"I'm counting on you two to take care of each other. Your mom's not herself right now and she needs you around her. Stress does funny things to people, and right now it helps her think Ryan's still alive." Ben winced inside but didn't try to contradict his dad. "As long as your mom stays in the mountains, she doesn't have to face the truth. I don't know how she'll react once we get back home. Do what you can to steer her in the right direction. You know what I mean don't you?" Ben knew what he meant. His dad wanted him to try and convince his mom that Ryan was dead. But how could he convince her when he didn't believe it himself? He gave none of these thoughts away when he answered his dad.

"We'll be fine Dad." Ted stared at his son's face and put his hand on Ben's shoulder.

"I know I'm asking a lot of you, but you do realize we won't be finding Ryan alive don't you?"

Ben ignored these words and it was all he could do not to shake his dad's hand from his shoulder. He felt

70

conflicted, and wanted to shout for his dad to leave, to go ahead and abandon them, but instead, he took a deep breath and told him what he wanted to hear. "I'm okay Dad." But in the next breath he reminded his father about the tasks he'd given him to do once he got home.

"Yes, I'll check with the Mill Hollow Police again on my way home. I'll contact the missing kid's hotline from home, and call Pastor Hurley to keep up the prayer chain. Have I forgotten anything?" His voice held a hint of sarcasm that was lost on Ben, who shook his head. "I've got other things to do back home too, like my job, and paying all the bills that are piling up at the Post Office. I can't stay here like the two of you, reading and playing chess, and pretend everything's okay." He let his hand drop from his son's shoulder.

"That's not all we'll do, Dad. We'll go out every day and search for Ryan and keep track of our movements. We'll cook and pray, and we'll…."

His dad interrupted, "You better not walk any further with me, I don't want you getting lost. Take care, Ben. You and your mom mean everything to me!" Ted's voice cracked and he turned away from Ben, each of them going their own way into different worlds with very different goals.

Chapter 15
July 16

Ryan's days took on a routine for him. First thing every morning, on his way back from the outhouse, or 'privy' as Amos and Lizzie Sue liked to call it, he'd put one more small rock under his mattress. He'd never gotten a straight answer as to how long he'd been in the loft before his first conscious thought, but he decided to count the days from his first trip to the privy. This morning's stone made seventeen. Almost three weeks since he'd been well enough to walk down the ladder on his own.

After breakfast he usually explored the woods, venturing further each day, but still careful to mark his way by bending twigs to act as guides. Nothing looked the least bit familiar to him, but he felt himself getting stronger on these walks. Just walking to the privy and trying to eat meals at the wooden table had tired him out in the beginning. Now that his ribs were healed he was no longer afraid to take deep breaths. He was sure that if he started out in a different direction each day he'd find something that would lead him back home, or at least back to the tents. Unfortunately Ryan had no idea that when Amos rescued him he'd carried Ryan, by horse, several hours away from where he'd first gotten lost.

Ryan liked to think of his family back at the campsite. He couldn't imagine them leaving the mountains without him, but he knew they'd have to get on with their lives at some point. It was this thought that scared Ryan more than anything. His family might be getting along without him much better than he was getting along without them.

When Ryan got tired of walking he rested beneath trees and listened to the stillness around him. It amazed him how clear the skies were, and how absolutely quiet it could get without the rush of traffic, cell phones, TV's and computers. At these times Ryan felt a certain peace, a oneness with the mountain, and he wanted to share it with Ben. He vowed that when he got back home – and he didn't doubt that he would – he'd get rid of some of the noise in his life.

Each night during dinner Ryan tried to make conversation with Lizzie Sue and Amos, but he never got much out of either one. He asked how he got there? When he could go home? How he could repay them, and a million other questions. Lizzie Sue harrumphed and Amos looked bewildered and said things like, "Ye *are* home, boy." Or, "Ye was lost and I found ye." These were the most frustrating conversations Ryan ever had, and he often left the table in tears, running to the safety of the loft. At these times he planned how to escape. How to leave for good on one of his walks in the woods and wander until he found something or someone else who could help him. But these dreams, planned in anger, always ended with the realization that he was more afraid of getting lost again and maybe dying out there this time, than of staying here for a while longer.

Some nights Ryan tried different approaches to his questions. He'd begin by talking about something he'd seen on one of his walks, like a fox that ran in front of him, or some rabbits that let him get close. Then he'd throw in something about wanting to bring his mom and dad up to meet them as soon as they helped him get home. Amos just shook his head and asked Lizzie Sue what the boy was talking about. Lizzie Sue was protective of Ryan and was able to settle Pa down in one-way or another. About this time in the conversations Ryan got so frustrated with the lack of answers that he'd bang his way up the six stairs to the loft. He managed to keep most of his fear and anger inside of him out of respect for these people because, as strange as they were, they *had* saved his life, and he owed them for that. But he didn't know how much more he could take of this place or these people. He was beginning to worry that Amos might not be all right in the head and that when he called him 'son' it wasn't just a term of endearment - it was like he really believed it.

Once he was settled in the loft the best time of Ryan's day began. He'd lie there on the picky mattress and listen to the scraping of Amos whittling, and Lizzie Sue's humming as she sewed something or got breakfast things ready for the morning. He knew he wouldn't be bothered anymore for the day and could relax and let his mind wander to his real family. First he'd think about his brother and imagine what he was doing right then. Ryan usually pictured Ben shooting hoops outside their garage, sleeping in his bag at camp, or playing video games in their bedroom. Then he'd drift over to his mom and dad. He liked thinking of them in the kitchen sharing a last cup of coffee and a few laughs before cleaning up after dinner. Once in a while he'd picture the four of them eating at Mario's, their favorite place for pizza. And just before drifting off to sleep he'd see himself walking into his bedroom and plopping down on his bed, facing his twin.

July 23

Amos still called him Charlie, which he hated. Lizzie Sue called him Boy, which was preferable to Charlie, and he called them Amos and Lizzie Sue. There was more wrong in this house than he could figure out. Yesterday, Lizzie Sue gave him two more old shirts that fit him perfectly, and later when he was outside he stopped to rest on a bit of fenced in land, not too far from the cabin. He noticed once again, the letters 'CRLE' carved into a wooden cross and something strange hit him. He wondered if this could stand for Charlie. He guessed these people probably couldn't read or write much, and if his guess was right, that meant Charlie was dead, and things were way too strange here. This realization sent a shudder through him and gave him new resolve to get away soon. He didn't want his name to end up spelled wrong on a wooden cross.

Almost a month ago, when Ryan first became aware of where he was, but still wasn't able to make it down the ladder; he wondered what these people did all day. While he recuperated he realized mountain living took a lot of hard work and energy. Amos was usually busy hunting, preparing, or curing the meat he'd shot or trapped that day. He frequently cut firewood, tanned hides, or fixed something that needed 'fixin' around the house. Amos also spent time everyday with his horse, Nearly, their cow, Billie, and the chickens. Lizzie Sue never stopped for more than a couple of minutes. Between gardening, cooking, canning, cleaning, sewing, and fussing she was always on the go.

On top of being confused and homesick, Ryan was also beginning to feel restless and useless. He didn't have TV to watch, Ben to talk to, a book to read, or even a ball to bounce and he was going crazy. So far, Lizzie Sue had managed to stop Amos from spending any time alone with Ryan, and for that Ryan would be eternally grateful. He had no desire to hunt, trap, or clean animals. And he didn't trust Amos like he did Lizzie Sue. She always came between the two of them, or had a ready excuse when Amos wanted Ryan to do chores or go hunting with him. So far Amos had given in to his wife's demands of 'healin' time for the boy, but Ryan sensed a lack of patience beginning to boil inside of Amos, like the slow rumble of thunder. Thunder still far enough away that you didn't have to stop playing outside and go inside, but all the same, you knew it was just a matter of time before the sky would open up and spit down rain. Ryan wasn't sure how much longer he had before Amos began to spit down rain.'

More and more he felt the need to remind himself that these people, weird as Amos was, had been very kind to him, had nursed him back to health and tried to make him as comfortable as possible. He also told himself that if they'd meant to do him harm they would've done it by now, wouldn't they? These thoughts came to a head while 26 calendar stones were under his mattress. He made up his mind that he'd spent the last night on a pokey mattress in a house with no bathroom, no toys, no pencils, or paper, not even a deck of cards. He'd get them to talk tomorrow, or he'd just take the horse and get as far away from them as possible. If he could just figure the right way out of here!

July 28

The next morning, as soon as Ryan awoke, he jumped out of bed and remembered that today was the day he'd get answers. *Tonight at dinner I'll make them understand that I really appreciate their help. I won't cry or get emotional. Now that I'm rested and healthy enough I need to go home. I'll get them to show me a safe way down this mountain.* Then he reminded himself to offer a reward. *Amos might like money. He'll probably jump at the chance to get more money than he'd ever seen before.* Ryan's whole body pounded with these thoughts as he shot down the first rungs of the ladder and jumped the last three.

The first time Lizzie Sue had seen him go down the ladder this way was the only time she'd ever called him Charlie. She'd said, "Charlie, I've tole ye a thousand times not ta jump off'n that ladder." Ryan remembered this because Lizzie Sue had looked embarrassed the moment she'd said it, and because of what Amos had said afterward; "Never mind yellin' at the boy Ma, it's good ta have the jumper back in the house." At the time Ryan thought that was a strange thing to say, about having the jumper back in the house *again*, but then everything Amos said seemed strange.

Ryan shook his head to clear it from the nagging feeling of Amos's anger. He continued priming the pump at the kitchen sink and splashed cool water on his face. Next he rinsed his mouth and took a long swallow of the cool mountain water. At first he hadn't liked the taste of the

77

mineral-rich water, but now he found himself drinking it often throughout the day. He dried his face on the same towel Lizzie Sue and Amos used, which kind of freaked him out in the beginning. *When I get home mom will have a heart attack when I tell her that I haven't brushed my teeth or taken a bath in over a month! But neither had Lizzie Sue or Amos, of course Amos was missing several of his teeth and he did smell kind of ripe!*

As usual, his breakfast was waiting for him on the table. A piece of cornbread, a small jar of honey and a bowl of hard, small, mountain berries. He knew where to get the milk. The cellar was just below the loft. He cleaned his dishes and then went searching for Lizzie Sue. He found her bent over out back weeding in the garden. An ancient hoe was lying against the wooden fence. "Good morning Lizzie Sue," Ryan said cheerfully.

"Mornin' boy. Did ye sleep good?" She asked this every morning.

"Yes, thanks, and I ate my breakfast." Ryan knew that would be her second question.

"Hmmph," she muttered and got back to tending her garden.

"Can I help?" asked Ryan, who was feeling in need of a distraction, something to take his mind off the conversation he was determined to have that night at dinner.

"Help weed?" she asked surprised. "Suit yerself. The beans kin use it." Lizzie Sue was standing in the peppers. Ryan looked around. There was a bountiful supply of vegetables, which made Ryan think it must be close to August by now. He saw corn and tomatoes that he

78

recognized and of course the peppers, but everything else just looked green.

"Okay, I give up. Where are the beans?"

"Ain't ye never bin in a garden afore Boy?"

"I've just never seen what things look like growing in a garden. My mom gets our vegetables from the grocery store. The beans we eat come out of a can or a plastic bag in the freezer."

"A freezer?" questioned Lizzie Sue. "Ye mean somethin' with ice in it?"

Ryan stood still and stared at Lizzie Sue who was still bent over the peppers. He realized two things at that moment. First, they were about to have a real conversation, no pretending he was Charlie, and second, and maybe even more important, Lizzie Sue knew very little, if anything, about life off the mountain.

"Freezers do have ice in them," Ryan responded to Lizzie Sue. "They're metal boxes that keep food frozen for a long time. It would be like putting snow around a piece of food until it got cold and hard all the way through."

"Well why would ye want a hard and cold bean? Don't make no sense ta me."

"No, it just makes the beans last longer until you're ready to cook them."

"Ain't that what cannin's fer? Where do ye put a freezer, in yer root cellar?"

"We don't have a root cellar."

"No root cellar? Are yer kin poor?"

"We aren't poor. We just don't need a root cellar because of freezers, grocery stores and refrigerators."

"Refriger – whats?"

"Look, Lizzie Sue if you show me where the beans are I'll tell you all about our kitchen."

The rest of the morning and well into the afternoon was spent with Lizzie Sue teaching Ryan about okra, Lima beans, carrots, potatoes, onions, beets, corn, peppers and tomatoes. He learned how to pick off bad bugs and squeeze them between his fingers until they popped, and which good bugs to leave alone. Ryan enjoyed the work so much that he never did get back to the refriger-what, and he and Lizzie Sue worked until it was almost time for Amos to get home.

After a supper of hot biscuits, venison stew and berry cobbler, Ryan helped Lizzie Sue with the dishes. He joked with her about the weeding today, setting up a good mood, to talk to them about his leaving and the reward money. He looked at Amos who'd been watching this with a frown on his face. "That's woman's work Charlie. If ye're fit enough ta weed and clean ye're fit enough ta hunt and chop. Tamorrow mornin' ye'll be with me, no more excuses!"

"Amos it's too soon," wailed Lizzie Sue.

"No Ma, it ain't. He seems fit enough and his mind's strong." Amos turned his attention to Ryan. "Charlie, it's time fer ye ta start callin' us by our rightful names agin'. No more of this Lizzie Sue and Amos. It ain't respectful and yer Ma and I brung ye up ta respect yer kin. From now on ye best call us Ma and Pa."

Ryan's head began to spin but his eyes were riveted on Amos who'd never looked so menacing. Lizzie Sue was standing still at the sink with her back to them. Time stopped in the cabin. Ryan became aware of his own breathing and of the crickets outside. "What?" was all he could manage?

"And while we're talkin' Charlie, no more of this, 'when are ye takin' me home?' Ye're home boy and yer Ma and I have waited a long time fer ye ta git back ta us. We jist want it ta be like it used ta be. First thin' tomorrow we're goin' huntin' Shoot us some rabbit fer supper."

"I don't know how to shoot rabbits. I don't *want* to shoot rabbits. I want to go home!" Ryan's voice was getting higher as he got more emotional. "I appreciate all you two have done for me, but my name's not Charlie, it's Ryan, and I have my own mom and dad! Please take me home!" He was almost crying now and his breath was coming in ragged gasps. Something was wrong here, even more wrong than he'd thought before. He looked pleadingly at Lizzie Sue's back.

She turned around and stepped in front of Ryan to talk to her husband. She looked up over a foot above her head to stare at his eyes. "Amos there's lots a thin's the boy cain't remember how ta do. He was haid sick fer a long time. Be gentle with him. Ye may have ta teach him some thin's all over agin. Why taday he didn't even know what okra was. Kin ye believe that?" Ryan knew Lizzie Sue was trying to help him, but he also sensed fear in what she was saying. What he couldn't hear were the thoughts going on in her head; *Amos this boy ain't Charlie, he don't know nothin' bout huntin' and trappin', and I'm afeared fer him and fer ye.*

Amos reached around his tiny wife and pulled Ryan in front of him. "There's one thin' I'm gonna teach ye agin right here and now Charlie and that's how ta respect yer kin." Amos slapped Ryan across the face with his left hand while letting him go with his right. Ryan spun across the

81

room like a toy top and fell into the door. Tears welled up in his eyes and he brought a hand to his face where it was stinging. He'd never been hit like that.

"What do ye call yer Ma?" Amos bellowed. Ryan looked at Lizzie Sue hoping that somehow this small woman could help him, but she just hung her head. "I'm waitin' Charlie!" Amos's hand was raised again and Ryan knew he'd make good the threat of another slap.

"Ma!" cried Ryan, not really sure if he was answering Amos's question or pleading for help. Lizzie Sue would have given anything to hear someone call her Ma again, but not like this. She moved to the kitchen sink and made herself finish the dishes.

"And what's my name boy?"

"Pa," answered Ryan weakly.

"Don't be fergettin' that agin. Now git ta bed cuz there ain't no more sleepin' late fer ye. Ye'll be up early tamorrow and I'll be teachin' ye a thin' or two 'bout these mountains."

That night in the loft Ryan replayed the dinner conversation a hundred times. *How had everything gone so wrong?* Each time he was left with the sickening conclusion that Amos really *did* think he was Charlie. Not in some 'Oh I wish my son was here so I'll take you' – but *really really* thought he *was* Charlie.

Ryan's mind flashed to the crudely carved CRLE cut into the pine cross on the hill past the garden. Even though these people couldn't read or write, could Amos have known enough letters to put part of Charlie's name on that cross? This thought scared him and yet why else were there clothes in the loft that fit him? And why did Lizzie Sue say she'd told him a thousand times not to jump down the ladder? A dozen other things came rushing back to him, like the time he heard Amos and Lizzie Sue whispering about him after he'd gone to bed. Amos had asked why Charlie was talking so fancy. Lizzie Sue replied, "A year's a long time ta be gone from yer Ma and Pa, and anythin' coulda happened in a year."

This had made no sense to him then, because he knew he couldn't have been gone from his mom and dad and Ben for a year. But it made some kind of horrible sense to him now. They thought, or at least Amos thought, he *really* was their dead son. *But if Amos believed Charlie had come back from wherever – the dead - after a year, then he really is psycho! And I'm supposed to go hunting with him tomorrow?*

Then Ryan had another thought that made him bolt up from the pokey mattress. *How did Charlie die?* And this thought led to other frantic thoughts. *I need to get out of here! I'll get up early and saddle Nearly and get away. It doesn't matter where. Nowhere can be any creepier than staying here and pretending I'm a dead boy named Charlie.* He fell back on the bed with a thud. *Who am I kidding? Thirty minutes away from our camp and I'd gotten hopelessly lost and almost died!* Ryan's thoughts continued racing. He could tell from the mountain elevation that he was much farther into the mountains than he'd been with his parents. His daily walks away from the house had not left him with anything familiar to follow. *So what's worse? Getting lost again or staying with crazy people?* He mentally made a list of the pros and cons of each plan, and was left more confused than before.

Maybe I can still offer Amos money. I never got a chance for that tonight. His hand went to his cheek, still stinging from Amos's hit. *How dangerous are these people? Is Lizzie Sue afraid of Amos too?* Ryan's mind started taking another route. *I'm bigger than Lizzie Sue, maybe...* But as badly as he wanted to get away from these people he couldn't see himself knocking out Lizzie Sue and stealing her hoe. There were two rifles above the door, and Amos always took just one with him. The other must have been Charlie's gun, but he didn't know how to load and shoot a rifle. On and on and on rambled his thoughts until finally Ryan drifted off into a nightmare of guns, bloody rabbits and Amos' big hands.

Chapter 16
August

Going hunting with Amos was just as miserable as Ryan thought it would be. Amos didn't like to talk, so Ryan tried to learn by watching. When he had to ask a question, like where the safety on the gun was, Amos spoke to him as if he was a baby. The first few times Ryan shot the gun he came home with a bruised shoulder. Up to this point he hadn't shot at anything living, but he knew it was just a matter of time before Amos expected him to bring something home. Ryan shuddered when he thought about that day.

Ted made the ten-hour drive from New York to Mill Hollow. He left work at noon, picked up supplies for Sarah and Ben and made it to the familiar parking spot on the mountain around midnight. He slept in the car for a few hours then hiked in to see his wife and son. He was exhausted from the week, the drive, the hike, and the worry. He was tired of trying to put on a happy face for them and he wasn't sure how much longer he could keep up this pace. When he was at work his mind was on the mountain. When he was on the mountain all he could think about was taking his family home and getting on with their lives. He was spread too thin and no one was getting the attention they deserved.

During Saturday reunions he expected no news of Ryan, but realized Sarah wanted him to ask, so he did. On the other hand, Sarah and Ben eagerly awaited any meager news from home. And then came the questions...Was Ryan listed as missing on the Internet? What did the FBI say? What did their friends say? Did he write their congressman? What about Senator Wilkins? Is he making any progress on getting a plane for them? It was becoming too much for Ted.

August 12

Ted stretched against the steering wheel as the alarm on his watch went off. He looked around at the trees surrounding his car and rubbed his face with his hands. This was the weekend he was going to take Sarah and Ben home. He hoped she wouldn't give him any trouble. It was a task he was looking forward to with mixed emotions. Just two nights ago he stood in his son's bedroom looking at the remains of a once vibrant life. The boys didn't need to share a bedroom but they insisted on it. Ben's half of the room, similar to Ryan's, didn't interest Ted as he concentrated on the other half. Soccer trophies, field day ribbons, music, wildlife and basketball posters, as well as drawings of super heroes and monsters adorned the walls. He wondered if he should take these things down. *Will Ben take more comfort in seeing something familiar, or will he not want to be reminded of Ryan everywhere he looks?* Ted was sure that if Sarah were given her way she'd leave the whole room just as it was forever, as a kind of shrine to Ryan. A tightness gripped Ted's chest and he walked out of the room, leaving everything in the same place, putting off the decision about Ryan's things until later.

This week, as Ted hiked up the mountain he went over the heart breaking summer. *I can't believe I was stupid enough to think this vacation would be the best thing we've*

ever done as a family. It'll be a vacation we'll never forget,
that's for sure. How am I supposed to make things right? It's
been weeks since Ryan left camp. No one, especially a 13
year old, could survive this long in the mountains without
help. Why can't Sarah see that?

Sarah, Ben and Ted settled around the campfire. It
was Saturday night and the next morning the three of them
would break camp for good. The mood was somber until Ted
broke the silence. "I finally got through to Senator Wilkins."
His voice sounded too loud in the quiet surroundings and he
was sorry he'd said it.

"What did he say?" asked Sarah, looking at her
husband.

"He doesn't think there's anything he can do."

"Nothing he can do?" whispered Sarah, shaking her
head. "What's he mean there's nothing he can do?"

"What did you expect Sarah?"

"I expected somebody besides Ben and me to be
concerned about a 13 year old boy who's gone missing,
that's what I expected!" Sarah's voice had gone from a
whisper to a shriek. Ted sensed she might lose it soon, but
couldn't think of anything to say. None of the little jingles he
was so good at coming up with at his advertising firm would
help, and that's all that was running through his mind. He
turned away from his wife and walked toward the tents.

"We're just going to have to take out a loan and rent
our own rescue planes," Sarah shouted after him. She said
this with such a matter of fact tone that Ted knew she'd been
thinking about it for a while. She was grasping at straws, at
least that's the way Ted saw it. She'd do anything to prolong

the search for Ryan, to put off leaving the mountains and returning to New York without her son. This was going to be the hardest thing his wife had ever done. He thought, *At least I've had the last few weeks to get used to the idea of Ryan not being at home. It's going to hit her hard once she steps inside the house.* He yearned to tell his wife that he understood how she felt. He wished he could tell her that he loved her, but most of all he wanted to tell her that everything would be okay. How could he do this when he wasn't sure he believed it himself?

Ted looked back at his wife, her eyes shining with her latest idea of how to get a search plane, and then to his son, looking so scared and vulnerable, and his heart sank to the bottom of his soul. Sarah had aged visibly. Her clothes hung on her and he saw gray hairs surrounding her deeply tanned face. *How can I tell her that a plane wouldn't do any good? How can I tell her that her dream of finding our son alive after all this time is just that, a dream? What does she expect to see anyway, a big SOS built out of rocks?*

He began softly, trying to reason with her, "Sarah, it won't work."

"It could Ted. We need to try!"

"Don't you think we should concentrate on getting you back to teaching and Ben ready to face eighth grade without Ryan?"

Sarah interrupted her husband and tried to bring Ben into the conversation. "You'd like to get a search plane wouldn't you Ben?" Ben wished he could melt into the background. It seemed like he was always siding with one parent or the other since Ryan disappeared. He couldn't remember the last time they'd all had fun.

Yeah, he thought, *we had fun the night before Ryan disappeared.* His mind wandered to that evening and he saw his parents laughing with their arms around each other. They'd all gone to bed satisfied and full of love, laughter, and the hope of a new day. He wanted to feel that way again, but he knew if Ryan didn't come back, things would never be as free and fun as it was that night. His parents were both looking at him, expecting some kind of answer to something, but he couldn't even remember what the question was. He stared into the fire.

Sarah went on, giving up on a response from her son. "You know the sheriff in Mill Hollow said there are people up here in the hills who've never even been off the mountains. They're born and raised here. That's what he said, maybe Ryan's with one of those people."

"That doesn't make sense Sarah. Why would Ryan stay with them? Why wouldn't those people bring him to Mill Hollow?"

"The Sheriff said the ones who come to town usually only go once or twice a year. They'll be coming soon to trade pelts and woodcarvings for winter supplies. I'm sure some will be down soon. We can't leave until these people go to town."

"You're wishing for something that won't happen, Sarah! Besides the sheriff will talk to these people when they come to town." Ted walked back to the fire.

"I could quit my job, or take a year's leave of absence. I'd have time to keep the search going."

"Doing what Sarah? We've been through all of this before. You've been here for weeks now and haven't come up with anything. Ben deserves some normal time too. If you

89

quit your job we need to sell the house and uproot the last of what feels good to him."

"Who needs normal time Ted? You or us?" It was at this point in the argument that tears started to quietly roll down Ben's face. He couldn't help it, they seemed to have a mind of their own, coming and going without his consent. He got up to go to the loneliness of his tent, knowing it would be more welcoming than staying here.

Ted looked at his wife with such anguish that Sarah was sorry she'd pushed so hard. He threw his coffee on the fire and stomped off to bed leaving his son to cry in his tent, and his wife to cry at the fire.

Ben lay on top of his brother's sleeping bag trying to decide what to do. Part of him wanted to run to his Dad and tell him that it would be okay, everybody would be happy again, that Ryan would come home. He wanted to make his dad believe, just like he was able to do with his mom. Even the tiniest feeling he got about Ryan throughout the day would lift her spirits. But, the other part of Ben knew his Dad wasn't interested in his connections to Ryan, so he stayed, frozen in his self-imposed blue prison, measuring 6' x 5'.

Soon Ben began to feel cold and unzipped the sleeping bag he'd been sitting on and snuggled down to breathe in the scent of his twin. He reminded himself that he'd know if Ryan was dead, because a part of him would be dead too. That part, the connection they shared as identical twins, and best friends was only sleeping, waiting for his twin's return. It wasn't waiting to find some sign of Ryan's death. He had no sense that Ryan was dead. In fact, there'd been times lately when he'd felt a strong connection, had felt

Ryan's fear. At other times he worried these feelings were only his own fears echoing back at him. Ben shook his head from side to side, and affirmed to himself, *No, Ryan's alive and not even hurt anymore, but he's still scared.* These thoughts, like most nights lately, put Ben to sleep.

Morning came all too soon for Sarah. She'd been up most of the night by the fire and in the early morning hours, had come to a decision her husband was not going to like. She wouldn't leave the mountain for ten more days, unless Ryan was found before then. Staying ten more days would still give her two days to get her classroom ready. She thought this decision would make Ben happy too. They'd become good at keeping track of their movements in a log, making sure they were back to the agreed upon spot by Friday night so Ted could find them. *What would I do if I went home? Cry with my friends? Roam around a too empty house?*

Chapter 17
August 18

Ryan awoke with a start and saw that it was still dark outside. He didn't feel like looking at his watch. He'd been dreaming one of those dreams that had no clear pictures, just intense, muddled feelings. The feelings were mainly of anger and guilt but they kept swirling around and around and seemed to have something to do with his parents, his brother, separation and tension. These emotions were mixed with other feelings of indecision, loneliness, and helplessness. That's when he woke up. When he was home and had a scary dream he woke Ben up to talk about it. His brother did the same thing. But here, in this uncomfortable loft, there was no sleeping brother. He calmed himself down by focusing on the fact that his Mom and Dad rarely argued, and that he had a happy family. But he also knew his foolish actions probably sent his family into chaos.

He rolled over, thankful for the feather pillow on this awful mattress. His thoughts wound back to how and when he'd get home. Just before he drifted off he rolled over onto his belly and stretched his hands under the mattress and counted 47 calendar stones. His last conscious thought was that Ben and his Mom would probably be starting school soon.

August 20
"Rise and shine, Charlie," boomed Amos's voice. "We're goin' huntin' agin."

Ryan bolted out of a deep sleep, forgetting where he was, and hit his head on the loft ceiling. When he saw Amos's face peering over the ladder his heart raced like a rapid-fire machine gun.

"Come on Boy! Ye gonna rub yer haid all day or are ye gonna git yer britches on and grab yer grub? I got yer gun."

As if in a trance, Ryan slid into his clothes, wishing for a shower. He went downstairs where Lizzie Sue was setting out a breakfast of bread, jelly and eggs. "Good morning Lizzie Sue," Ryan said on his way to the privy. He realized his mistake as soon as it came out, and he froze, hoping he wouldn't get a bruised cheek this time. It never would have happened, slipping up like this, if he hadn't gotten off to such a bad start this morning.

"What'd I tell you 'bout callin' me and yer Ma by our rightful names?"

"It don't matter what he calls me Pa, hush up and let the boy be." Amos sulked off to his place at the table and told Ryan to hurry out to the privy and get back to the table.

Back inside the house Ryan wasn't sure he could eat anything. He saw two guns gleaming in the corner by the door. His parents wouldn't even allow him and Ben to have a paint ball gun and now Amos expected him to kill something with one. Ryan's stomach churned and turned sour as he swallowed a mouthful of runny eggs.

"Let's git Charlie. We're goin' after some rabbits taday."

Ryan shuddered involuntarily as he remembered the pet rabbit Sneakers that he and Ben had gotten when they were six years old. Sneakers lived in a cage in their garage for three years until he died. Sneakers walked on a leash with the boys and came when he was called. Ryan went white at the thought of shooting and eating a relative of Sneakers.

Lizzie Sue watched Ryan during breakfast. She saw him lose his color, but knew there was nothing she could do to help. "Remember, Pa, he'll need remindin' agin on how ta kill a animal. It's not like the shootin he bin doin'. He was hurt bad and these things take time ta heal." Lizzie Sue hated herself for playing into this scene, but she was lonely for 'Charlie' too, and Pa had been so much happier lately. Her heart was torn in two with conflicting feelings ever since Amos brought the boy home.

"He's doin' fine," answered Amos, slapping Ryan on the back, and almost dislodging the egg Ryan was trying to get down. Ryan felt like his breakfast was in his throat as he walked outside. Nearly was saddled and ready to go. Ryan clumsily hoisted himself up on the horse, wondering how early Amos got up, and then he wondered how Amos told time. There was no clock in the house except for Ryan's watch, and he was careful not to let Amos see it. He checked it now, 5:57 a.m. He couldn't remember being awake this early. He looked around him from the vantage point of sitting on Nearly and couldn't help being impressed by the morning light coming through the trees. The quiet, the colors, and the earthy smells, called out to Ryan as he prepared himself for whatever lay ahead.

Amos stuck the two shotguns in the saddle and mounted Nearly. "We'll have ta git ye a horse fer yer own Charlie. Maybe Jack'll trade us fer a calf the next time his mare drops a colt."

94

This was bizarre. Ryan had always wanted a horse, what kid didn't dream of a horse of their own? But getting one like this? Then a bright thought hit him; *maybe I could use that horse to help me get away! It'd be easier than trying to steal Nearly.* Just as soon as this thought lit up his morning he realized that getting a colt, and raising it was a long way off and he couldn't wait that long to escape. Still, it left him feeling a little less adrift with no plan. He rubbed his watch underneath the flannel shirt like a talisman; something he did often. It was his last link to anything modern and not of this mountain. *Too bad,* he thought once again, *that I didn't bring my other watch, the one with the day and date, alarm and compass!*

They'd been riding for about half an hour when Amos got off Nearly. He told Charlie to jump down and get his gun. When Ryan reached for one of the two guns in Nearly's saddle Amos hissed, "Not that one!" Ryan quickly reached for the other. He was still impressed by how heavy it was. It felt cool and smooth and powerful. He held it carefully, not handling it with any expertise. Amos loosely tied Nearly to a tree and took off walking with his gun. Ryan followed, slinging the gun over his shoulder as Amos had done. The mountain air was crisp and held a hint of a breeze. Then it hit him; a thought so powerful that he actually had to stop walking for a second. *I could shoot Amos! I could shoot him, get on Nearly and take off!* It was such a simple and yet terrifying thought that he was paralyzed. The thought, *kill him, kill him,* was searing his brain. It was only a gruff whisper from Amos that brought him back to reality. A reality in which he knew he could never shoot anyone.

"There Charlie!" Amos was pointing to his left at three small brown rabbits. Ryan smiled at the peaceful animals nibbling away. "Shoot Charlie!" whispered Amos. "Git our supper fer Ma." Ryan froze. "Shoot!" whispered Amos a little more forcefully. Amos noticed the look of panic on Ryan's face and mistook it for confusion. Remembering what Ma had said, Amos walked behind Ryan, grabbed the rifle from him and positioned it against Ryan's shoulder. He clicked off the safety and whispered, "Jist pull the trigger."

"I can't Amos!" cried Ryan, knowing he'd made a mistake as soon as it came out of his mouth. Amos lifted the rifle from Ryan and shot it, killing one of the rabbits on the run before it had a chance to escape.

"No!" Ryan cried out. And then, fast as lightning, Amos swung around and backhanded Ryan. The crack of a broken nose resounded in Ryan's ears. He stumbled back several feet and fell down. Tears stung his eyes and rolled down his cheeks. His hands flew to his nose, which was bleeding profusely. It hurt to cry, but he couldn't stop. He was dizzy and scared, and tasted blood in his mouth. The thought of killing Amos crossed his mind again. *"I should have killed him when I had the chance!"*

"What's my name Charlie?"

"Pa," answered Ryan weakly.

"What boy? I cain't hear ye!"

"Pa!" shouted Ryan through his sobs.

"And don't ye fergit it! Now git that rabbit. The next one is yers!" Ryan started shaking his head no. He couldn't possibly pick up the dead rabbit. But he noticed Amos's face, dark as a winter's night, so he moved forward, wiping blood on his shirtsleeve. His head was throbbing, his nose hurt more than anything had ever hurt before, and even though he took his time getting to the rabbit and told himself that the rabbit wasn't Sneakers, he still couldn't look at it. He turned and squatted, holding his head erect and still. With his right hand cupping his nose he began to feel blindly around on the ground with his left. His hand grazed some warm sticky fur and he looked against his will. The rabbit was laying on its side, stretched fully out. Blood wetted the soft brown fur around several holes made by the shot. Ryan thought he was going to lose the runny egg from this morning's breakfast.

He looked at the rabbit, summoning the courage to pick it up. He let go of his nose and scooped it up with both hands. As he took his hand away from his nose drops of his blood mingled with the rabbits. He felt things he'd never felt before, dark, angry things. Things he wasn't equipped to handle. His head ached, his nose throbbed, he was covered in blood and he felt every minute as young and inexperienced as his thirteen years. He'd never wanted his mother so much in his whole life. He wanted to be sitting on her lap; he wanted to be hearing her say she loved him and everything was going to be okay. When he sensed Amos approaching he held the rabbit out and away from him, pressing it towards Amos.

Amos grabbed the rabbit by the ears saying, "This is the way ye hold it. What's wrong Charlie? Have ye forgotten everthin' I lairned ye?" Amos was quieter now, almost gentle again, and this note of tenderness confused Ryan. Here he was, in the woods with a man who thinks he's his dad. A man who expects him to kill animals and enjoy his

97

company, and the real Charlie would have loved this alone time with his dad. The darkness Ryan felt a few minutes ago was replaced by a pang of something like tenderness. His emotions were ping ponging all over the place and he couldn't gain control of them.

Maybe it was the look on Ryan's face as Amos grabbed the rabbit out of his hands, or maybe it was something else. But whatever it was, Ryan was grateful that Amos didn't make him shoot anything else that morning. Amos shot four additional rabbits before they headed home. The ride, high atop Nearly, was excruciating. Ryan's nose throbbed and crusted over with blood. He was having a hard time breathing and could hardly wait to get back to Lizzie Sue. Surely she'd know how to make his nose feel better.

If Ryan thought shooting a rabbit was bad, it was nothing compared to what Amos wanted him to do with the rabbits once they were back at the cabin. Amos shouted, "Hey!" to Lizzie Sue and she called back, happy to see the boy again until she saw his bloodied nose and shirt.

"What happened Pa?" she asked shakily. "Not another!"

"Nothin' ta fret over, Ma. Charlie jist needed some remindin' on how ta be respectful."

Ma helped the boy off Nearly and took his head in both her hands, turning it this way and that. She touched it gingerly and the boy winced and backed off. "He needs me ta care fer it."

"Not until he's cleaned these rabbits first," ordered Amos. Lizzie Sue let go of Ryan's face and told him to git. Ryan reached for her hand, not wanting to be alone with

Amos again, but she pulled it back and turned toward the house with a heavy heart.

At the barn Amos took the rabbits off Nearly. They were all bound together around the necks by a dirty old rope. Amos sat on a crude bench attached to the wall of the barn. He took out his knife and faster than Ryan would have thought possible he gutted and skinned the rabbit. Next, he used the tip of the blade to dig out the shotgun pellets and handed the knife to Ryan.

"Finish here while I git Nearly out ta pasture and see ta gittin' the skins ready."

Ryan's mouth fell open but the sting of Amos's blow to his nose and his bruised cheek reminded him of what Amos could do if provoked. Ryan took the bloody knife and Amos turned to leave. *What had Amos done first? Somehow cut a long slit in the belly and thrown the guts in a bucket.* Ryan gingerly picked up a rabbit, laid it across the bench next to him and took a deep breath through his mouth, feeling somewhat lucky for not being able to smell the dead rabbits.

He pierced the skin with the tip of his knife. *Where did Amos, Pa, cut from, bottom up or top down? Does it even matter?* Ryan took a guess and thrust the knife deep into the rabbit's belly. It was soft and gave more resistance than cooked chicken and he gagged. *Don't think of the rabbit as Sneakers. It's just dinner, it's like mom going to the supermarket and getting chicken.* When he tried to slice the rabbit's chest he realized he had the knife in too deep because it had gone clear through the rabbit and was sticking into the bench. It was then that Ryan doubled over and threw up. This started his nose bleeding again. He spit and wiped his mouth on his shirt and tried again to gut the rabbit. He made a mess of it; all the while worried that Pa would catch him still on his first rabbit. Ryan was barely holding it together and had never missed his family as much as right now.

Luckily it wasn't Pa who rounded the corner of the small barn, but Ma. She looked at the knife in the boy's hand, the panicked look on his bloodied face, the crude cut in the rabbit's belly, and the morning breakfast on the ground. "Gimme that knife boy." Deftly she took care of the remaining rabbits while Ryan watched. "Leave the skins," directed Lizzie Sue who was gathering the dead animals in her apron. Bring the bucket of innards."

Ryan gratefully picked up the bucket. "Thanks, Ma," he said as he trotted alongside of her, and for once didn't even mind calling her Ma.

Ma, Lizzie Sue's heart jumped for joy as she pondered this word. *Maybe it will be okay after all. The boy kin have a good life here once he gits the flow a things.* "Let's see ta your nose afore dinner." Ryan, who craved some sign of warmth or compassion for his situation almost hugged the little woman. Instead, he followed her inside the house and tried not to cry while she cleaned, packed, and tended to his broken nose.

Pa grumbled a little at dinner that night when he was served dried venison and not the rabbit stew he wanted, but Ryan would be eternally grateful for Lizzie Sue's kindness.

Pa left Ryan alone for the next few days because Ma told him the boy's nose needed to heal. It was during these days of healing, while he was helping Lizzie Sue in the

100

garden, and tending to the animals, that he grew to have strong feelings for the woman with the frizzy red hair. She tended to Ryan's nose with herbs and flowers in her worn doctoring bag. She hummed quietly while she prepared meals, and sometimes Ryan caught her staring at him with a smile on her lips. After all this time away from his family Ryan lived for these little smiles and the kindness behind Lizzie Sue's hands checking his nose, and the melodies in her humming. He drank it up like a newborn pup lapping at his mother.

Chapter 18
August 23

Ted pushed the button on his watch to quiet the buzzing. The noise told him it was time to wake up and make his way to Sarah and Ben, who would both be sleeping in the bigger tent. Weeks ago he'd thought it was fitting and somehow symbolic that he was the one to sleep alone in the pup tent early Saturday mornings when he arrived back at the campsite. *It's two against one no matter what I do these days.*

This is it, he thought as he trekked alone under the full moon. *If I never see this place again it will be okay with me.* He was tempted to just leave the tents and all the camping equipment. Let it rot, or let some lucky hiker who happened by have it all. He was never going to use it again. But he knew Sarah wouldn't agree to leave it, and somehow Sarah had been the one to call the shots since Ryan's disappearance. *No more though. There's no more time to talk me into leaving them here. We need to get on with things and she's got to see it's the best for Ben too. School starts in less than a week and life without Ryan begins.*

Ted was glad to see the pup tent and was asleep as soon as his boots were off and his head hit the sleeping bag.

Things were quiet in the morning. Sarah didn't come into kiss him awake; Ben didn't hug him when he came out of the tent. He was the big bad guy making them leave the mountains. The one who was taking them 500 hundred miles away from the last living tie they had to Ryan. *Well, if this is how it's got to be, then so be it. I can play the bad guy for a while longer.* He pitched in taking down the tents and packing up with barely a nod to his family. He was not looking forward to ten hours in the car with this silent treatment.

        The Jeep pulled into the garage at 10:42 p.m. Sunday night. It had been 56 days since Ben or Sarah had seen their home and 48 days since they'd seen Ryan. No one said a word as the door rolled down with a shudder, making the garage feel like a prison cell being locked for the night. The faint light from the door opener showed Ted exactly how hard this was going to be on his wife and he mustered all the love he could for her as he got out of the car and went around to her side. He opened her door at the same time Ben opened his. Ted reached in to take his wife's hand but she shrugged it away. "I'm fine Ted. I don't need your help." Ben winced at the harsh sound of his mother's words. He slammed his car door harder than was necessary and everyone made their way into the house.

        Sarah dropped her bag in the mudroom and turned the kitchen light on. The house was bigger than she remembered, or was it just emptier? Her mind raced with a million thoughts: school started Wednesday, which gave her only two days to get her bulletin boards up, room ready, and lesson plans done. Ben needed new clothes and a haircut, there were mounds of laundry to be done, groceries to be bought, and a thousand other things that she didn't want to think about. Life back here couldn't be normal, not with her heart still on the mountain. All she wanted to do was take a hot shower and shut things out for a few more hours by sleeping in a real bed.

Sarah went back once to the garage to drag things out of the Jeep and then left the rest for Ben and Ted. Climbing the stairs to her room she caught sight of the twin's elementary school pictures hanging on the stairway wall. These pictures broke through her calm and she fell in a heap on the top step, burying her head in her hands and heaved great soul wrenching sobs. On the mountain she'd been able to keep hope alive that Ryan would be found, but now hope seemed a million miles away, and everywhere she looked were reminders of Ryan; pictures, toys, books, clothes, and memories. How could she go on? She slammed her fists into the carpeted steps.

Ben rounded the corner from the kitchen to start up the stairs and saw his mother crumpled in a pile at the top of the stairs. He couldn't read the expression on her face, but he knew how she felt. He started up the stairs and began talking without looking directly at her or the pictures on the wall. "It's strange, isn't it Mom? You look at me and want Ryan? I mean what else could you think besides where's the other one?"

Sarah's heart froze but she got up to go to her son. "No, Ben! I look at you and I see you, just like I always have! It's this house, it's being off the mountain. It's life going on without Ryan, and it scares me." Sarah's voice cracked and she covered her face with her hands.

"But Mom, we believe Ryan's coming back! We know he's safe. We know it! You told me we were a team, and that we'd never give up!" The fear was evident in Ben's wavering voice. *Is mom losing faith?* His mind barely let that thought creep in, but once it was there it was hard to ignore. It was this moment, above all others that hastened Ben's downhill spiral of depression and defiance. Stomping up to his room he cried, "I don't care what you do, I'm never giving up!"

Ted stood at the bottom of the stairs holding backpacks and other odds and ends from the car. He didn't realize it, but he was also holding his breath, waiting for his wife's reaction. He knew her response would set the tone for the next few days. Sarah reached out to the empty spot Ben had just left. "Oh Ben, how can I say what I feel? I want to believe, I really do," she cried, "but I've lost it! It's gone, my hope's gone! It melted away as soon as I got in the house." She dropped her hand, hating to be the cause of the hurt on her son's face. She looked down the stairs and focused on her husband. He met her look with the hint of a smile and Sarah wondered if it was because of the relief he felt at getting his family home, or happiness at what she'd just confessed to her son. Either way, she didn't like what she saw, and looked away from him.

In the next instant Ted dropped the things he was holding and raced up the stairs to put his arms around his wife. *Finally, she's facing things. She's coming back to reality.* Ted closed his eyes and let in a feeling of relief. He held his wife on the stairs, halfway to their son's bedroom, and let her cry herself out.

Ben stood inside the doorway of his bedroom and left the light off. He couldn't bear to look at the empty bed. Feeling the absence of Ryan was bad enough he didn't need to look at it too. He lay down on his bed, fully clothed, and went deep inside himself, summoning the invisible thread with millions of nerve endings that connected him to his twin. An immediate sense of calm came over him. Ryan *was* still there, inside of him. He *was* safe and he knew they'd be together again one day.

It was late at night, Ryan's favorite time of the day. The cabin was dark and quiet and he was in the loft, alone with his thoughts. There was no pretending to be Charlie, no hunting, trapping, or skinning. No fear that Amos would hit him. There was just calm, and being alone with his thoughts. Ryan closed his eyes and reached out to his twin. "Goodnight," he whispered. "Don't give up on me."

Chapter 19
August 31

Lizzie Sue walked to a plot of land fenced off with whittled pine sticks. The morning air was crisp and the sky was clear when she stopped in front of the cross marked CRLE. She drew her black knitted shawl closer around her body and let her mind wander to Ryan. *I know the boy hates huntin', but he's gittin' better at it. These last few weeks everthin's been calm and peaceful-like. Huntin's the mountain way a life and this **is** the boy's life now. He kin 'most gut and skin a squirrel nearly good as ye used ta, Charlie.* The name still made Lizzie Sue's heart ache and all the pretending in the world wouldn't make it go away.

Sometimes Lizzie Sue thought of the boy's own Ma and wondered if her heart was breaking too? She knew she wouldn't wish that hurt on anyone. She wondered why his folks never came for him. She knew they weren't mountain folk but she couldn't imagine why they didn't want him back? Some days she made up stories about his family all being dead, which made it okay that she and Amos were the only family the boy had. She liked these thoughts and could almost convince herself they were real. At these times she told herself if this were true, then staying on the mountain would be the best for him. She even told herself that he was young enough to get used to the idea that she and Amos were his parents. These thoughts came some days, on other days she fretted that someone would see Ryan and ask questions. She worried that his family wasn't dead and were still looking for him. Then she worried that letting Pa believe the boy was Charlie was wrong when she knew their son was dead. On these days she worried herself sick about what might happen and it took a lot of praying to shake those thoughts out of her head.

She looked at the plot of land where her and Amos' kin were buried. It was a pretty place and she kept flowers at all the graves. Amos used to whittle things for their cemetery before Charlie died. Now he never even looked this way, even though it was but 30 or so yards from the house. The sun was shining brightly on the mound of dirt and grass where Charlie lay buried. Ma knelt before the cross. It was made of pine, cut from the mountain trees not far from their house. Pa had taken care to carve fanciness around the cross, and in the middle he'd put the letters CRLE. They were all he knew how to write of his son's name. She prayed, *I still miss ye son, but ye're gone ta us forever, ain't ye?* Lizzie Sue wiped a tear away from her cheek. *There's somebody stayin' with us now. Pa brung him home when he was real sick. I nursed him back ta health. He's a good boy Charlie and he's keepin' me and Pa company. Pa calls him Charlie, and he do look a little like ye.* She sighed and bent her head forward before continuing her thoughts. *Pa never did git over the grievin' sickness for ye. Some days he's worse'n others but the new boy makes it better fer Pa. This youngen's name is Ryan, but Pa don't seem ta know it, he thinks it's ye Charlie, and I ain't got the heart to git him ta see ye're still in this hill. Watch over that youngen Charlie. He ain't did nothin' wrong 'cept maybe gittin' lost up here in the mountains from his true family.* She touched the wooden cross and closed her eyes for a few seconds before getting to her feet and walking back to the house. She had chores to do.

Later, in the midst of her chores, Lizzie Sue was still thinking about Ryan. *What would some of the neighbors think if they come by and saw the boy?* She primed the pump at the kitchen sink and her eyes wandered again to the pine cross. *They'd think Pa'd gone plum soft in the haid and I'd followed him.* Lizzie Sue smiled at herself. Each day there seemed to be more to smile about. *Having a youngen around the house has a way of healin' the brokenest heart.*

"Morning Ma," said a sleepy Ryan coming down from the loft.

"Mornin' boy. Breakfast's on the table. Pa let ye sleep in today. He's already gone." Ryan's heart leapt at the prospect of a whole day away from Amos. Amos hadn't hit him again since the first rabbit hunt, but the mixture of fear, grudging respect and pity that Ryan felt for him was confusing. It was much easier with Lizzie Sue because, unlike Amos, she seemed to accept him for who he was without really saying so.

"What can I help you with today, Lizzie Sue? Ryan had purposely called her by her name instead of Ma. He held his breath to see what her reaction would be. She gave him a glance, but made no comment. He'd tested her and that was a start.

"Sit down and eat boy."

"My name's Ryan you know."

"I knows yer name boy, and mind ye ta know mine when Pa's around."

It was suddenly very important for Ryan to hear someone call him by his real name. All he'd heard was 'Boy' or 'Charlie' for such a long time. "Can't you please call me Ryan? You could do it just when Amos is gone."

Her heart went out to the boy, to Ryan, but she couldn't soften too much. What good would that do? Pa would never let him go. She didn't know how to help him. She'd never been off the mountain. Pa was the one to go to town and to go trading with the neighbors. That's the way he liked it, so that's the way it was, and she never gave it much thought. Life was what it was on the mountain and she'd never been one to question it, or her husband.

"Won't do no good, boy. Now eat. We got soap ta make. Ye was still mountain sick when we took our last bath. It's bath time agin and Pa likes fresh soap. He's kinda fancy that way. No old soap fer him when it's bath time." Lizzie Sue actually smiled when she said this.

"We're gonna *make* soap? Ryan asked. "I never even thought about how soap was made."

"What did yer kin use fer soap?"

"We used regular soap, but we didn't make it. We bought it already made at the store."

"Soap already made! Now that sounds fancy." Lizzie Sue stoked the fire. A pot with some melting fat was already hanging over it. Looking at the familiar sight of Lizzie Sue stirring a pot made Ryan lonelier for his family, friends, and school. He also recognized something inside of him; a reluctant enthusiasm for the education he was getting on the mountain. He told himself that everything he learned would one day help him leave this mountain and survive the journey. But lately it was more than that. Even though he hated Amos shooting animals, and gutting them was really gross, he felt a certain thrill knowing dinner was coming from the mountains and not the supermarket. This was the way people had lived for thousands of years and he felt proud to be a part of it.

There was a naturalness to life on the mountain that felt good in a way that going to the grocery store never had. When he helped in the garden, Lizzie Sue taught him when the vegetables were ready to be picked and how much they had to 'lay by' for winter. He learned to salt and cure meats, and how to tan hides for trading in Mill Hollow. He learned some of the names of plants and herbs and how Lizzie Sue used them. This was far more than he learned earning his Boy Scout badges. Ryan's heart was conflicted because even though he enjoyed his time with Lizzie Sue, escape, like his twin, was never far from his mind.

His latest plan to get away involved talking Amos into taking him to town when he went for his yearly trip, which had to be coming up soon because fall was underway, and he'd heard Amos talking to Lizzie Sue about town. Of course he'd have to butter Amos up and remember to call him Pa and act – well act like Charlie. A few weeks ago he *had* asked Amos if he could go to town with him, but Amos told him no and Ryan hadn't brought it up again. He *would* bring it up again soon, and when he did he wouldn't take no for an answer. Ryan knew that once he got into town he could make someone listen. To get Amos to change his mind he would also need Lizzie Sue's help. Today was the perfect day to start working on that part of his plan.

Ryan cleaned his dishes and joined Lizzie Sue at the fireplace. He started telling her about soap at his house. "The soap we use at home is green and smells like flowers. It comes wrapped in a shiny box and it's called 'Irish Spring'."

"Green soap? With a name?" The things the boy told her when they were alone amazed her. In her mind she thought of the dark green of trees, not the paleness of the soap. "Does it make ye green when ye scrub with it?" Lizzie Sue laughed at the image.

"No more than your soap makes you white." Lizzie Sue seemed to ponder this for a while. "Do you know how we wash dishes at home?" Ryan asked.

"With pink soap," offered Lizzie Sue, with a smile at the corner of her lips.   "Lizzie Sue, is that a joke?"

"I don't know," she answered honestly. "Amos ain't one fer jokin'. Now when I was growin' up my Pa and Ma believed in laughin'. I don't think we laughed enough when Charlie was with us."

Ryan took a deep breath and asked, "What happened to Charlie?"

"This ain't a day fer talk like that boy. Tell me how yer kin washes dishes."

Ryan didn't want to push her for details so he dropped the subject of Charlie's death and went on to explain dishwashers to Lizzie Sue. "We take the dishes from the table when they're all dirty from eating and we put them in a metal box about this big." Ryan gestured with his hands. "You have to stack all the dishes with room around them so water and soap can swirl all over." Lizzie Sue was staring at Ryan with rapt attention and Ryan was enjoying teaching her something for a change. "The door has two little holes in it. We put liquid soap in both of the holes; then we close the big door on the front and push a button. Water heats up and swirls around on the inside of the box and mixes with the soap and the dishes get clean. The box drains the dirty water and rinses them with clean water. Finally, a little electric heater- something that's hot but without fire-dries the dishes. About an hour later the dishes come out clean, dry and warm."

"An hour ta do dishes!" The box and the button were lost on Lizzie Sue because she couldn't imagine wasting an hour out of her day on dishes.

"You can do other things while the dishwasher is working. It does all the work by itself, you don't have to stand there." Ryan couldn't believe he and Ben used to think it was so unfair when they had to do dishes. When he got home he'd gladly load the box and push the button. "I can't believe I'm talking about a dishwasher. I'm missing a dishwasher! Lizzie Sue do you know how it feels to have everything in your life turned upside down?"

"A course I do, boy," Lizzie Sue answered softly.

"I don't think you do! I miss my family every day, every minute! You don't know how it feels to miss someone like that?" Ryan looked at Lizzie Sue's pale face and wanted to bite his tongue as soon as he'd said it. Of course she knew what it was like to miss somebody! Her only son was dead.

"Yes boy, I know how it feels. I wouldn't want no one else ta have that ache in their heart, or the ache in their haid like Pa had afore ye come to us."

"But I didn't come to you! I got lost and you helped me get better." Ryan grew agitated as he grabbed Lizzie Sue's arm, "And I'll always be thankful for that, but I need to go now, can't you see that? *My* mother's heart is breaking just like yours."

"Cain't ye see how happy ye've made Pa? And even my heart ain't been so heavy lately. Don't me and Pa help ease yer longin' a little?"

Ryan shook his head, "It's not the same, Lizzie Sue. This life isn't my life. My life is with my brother and my mom and dad, my friends and school, and music, and soccer. It's my last year in middle school and I'm missing it. I want books and TV and all sorts of things you can't even imagine." Ryan's voice broke and he blinked back tears.

Lizzie's heart broke for the boy, but even more than this, something occurred to her that she'd never thought about before; "Ye know words boy?"

"What do you mean?" asked Ryan wondering where this question was coming from. He wiped a tear away with his, no, *Charlie's*, shirt.

"Words, kin ye make out words Boy?" Lizzie Sue was more animated than he'd seen her before.

"Do you mean read?" But Lizzie Sue was already off to the curtained room that she shared with Amos. Ryan had never seen the inside of this room before, and he didn't know if he should follow Lizzie Sue or not.

"Come here, boy," she ordered from behind the curtain. She was on her hands and knees pulling a box out from underneath a bed. A real bed, noted Ryan, with a feather mattress and a frame carved by Amos. It was high off the floor and a couple of steps were by the side so Lizzie Sue didn't have to jump from the bed. The spread was an array of colors and had been hand quilted by Lizzie Sue from scraps of whatever she found. The box Lizzie Sue pulled out was an old cardboard produce box brought back from one of Amos's trips to Mill Hollow.

114

Lizzie Sue plopped the box on the bed and threw the top off. It sank into the feathers a few inches. She remained kneeling on the floor in front of it, so short that she was barely able to see inside. She pawed through the contents like a puppy after a bug in the sand.

Ryan walked into the room and looked at Lizzie Sue with a smile. She was an interesting lady and he couldn't help but like her. Inside the box was an assortment of odds and ends: a couple of pieces of folded calico material, some spools of thread with needles stuck in them, a square of broken light blue glass, some baby clothes, several balls of yarn and some knitting needles, a jar of buttons and coins, a couple of pencils, an old plate, and something square wrapped in lace. She grabbed the lace-wrapped package and turned around sit down with the bed supporting her back. Ryan came and sat down on the floor, next to her. As she flipped through pages Ryan could see that it was an old Bible. She stopped on a page with several names written in large, childish script and mostly spelled wrong. The last name entered was CRLE.

"Kin ye put Charlie's name in the Bible? I worry so that it ain't proper. Pa did the best he kin, but kin ye do better? This Bible's bin in my family longer'n I kin remember."

Ryan turned around and picked out one of the pencils from the box. He took the Bible from Lizzie Sue and asked her what she wanted him to write.

"Charlie Riley. No, put Charles Riley. That's his proper name."

Ryan carefully erased the CRLE. "Did Charlie have a middle name?" asked Ryan before beginning to write, "I see that some of the others in here have middle names."

"He had my Pa's name for his middle name," she answered. Ryan waited with the pencil poised over the now blank line. "Charles Ryan Riley," she whispered.

"But Lizzie that's my name!"

"I told ye I know'd yer name boy and now I spoke it fer ye. But don't 'spect me to say it agin cause it'd set Pa off."

It was the first time Ryan had heard someone other than himself say his name in a long time and he liked the sound of it coming from Lizzie Sue. The feel of the pencil in his hand felt good too. He wrote 'Charles Ryan Riley' in cursive, as neatly as he could; neat enough he was sure to have made Mrs. Kelly, his fourth grade teacher, proud. He showed Lizzie Sue the words and she traced them with her finger. Ryan was about to close the book when he asked Lizzie Sue if she'd like him to read some of the words to her.

"Oh I got them names all in here,' she said pointing to her head. "My cousin Pete used ta be the keeper of the Bible, cuz he knew words, but I got it when Pete died."

"I don't mean the names, I mean the stories," answered Ryan.

"Do ye know *all* them words boy?"

"Most of them, and a whole lot more," said Ryan laughing. He opened to the first page of Genesis, and began to read. He read for a long time. It felt good to be holding a book and Lizzie Sue was in awe of it. Her eyes were closed but she listened intently, sometimes with a tear escaping from under the lid, and sometimes quietly reciting almost the same words Ryan was reading.

Ryan held the Bible on his legs, which were folded under him. He'd moved so that his back was against the wall, but Lizzie Sue was still leaning against the bed. He felt like they could have gone through the whole Bible if his voice held out. They went on like this for quite a while until they heard Amos yelling for them. Ryan and Lizzie Sue both jumped up like two kids who'd been caught with their hands in the cookie jar. Lizzie Sue knew Amos wouldn't take kindly to her sitting around all day listening to words instead of making soap for their bath.

"Git," she told Ryan, taking the Bible from his lap. "See ta what he wants." Ryan raced out of the bedroom and was outside with Amos before he got off Nearly. Amos threw two wild turkeys at him. He caught them, but the weight of the birds nearly knocked him off his feet. Amos laughed and Ryan smiled back.

"We kin start savin' feathers fer a real mattress fer ye Charlie. And we'll have us some turkey tamorrow. Ain't nobody makes turkey better'n yer Ma. She knows jist what herbs the turkey wants ta be cooked with." Ryan walked with the two birds to the barn, marveling at their size, the heads dragging on the ground. He laid them on the bench and waited for Amos, *Pa*, to teach him how to clean a turkey.

PART THREE
- SURVIVAL -

Chapter 20
October 8

Sarah found herself staying at school later and later. She talked herself into believing that Ted and Ben didn't need her at home. Ted barely noticed what she cooked anymore and half the time the family meal ended in an argument. There were times when Ben wasn't home for dinner, something she never would have allowed before. *How have things gotten bad so fast?* At first, friends at school had been supportive, but after a few weeks when they deemed it was time for her to get on with life they'd backed away from her. Try as she might, Sarah's timeline for grieving the disappearance of her son, wasn't the same as theirs. The only one who still tried to talk with her about Ryan was her best friend Sheila. At least three or four times throughout the day Sheila popped into her classroom just to say hi, or to bring her a cup of coffee or a hug. She didn't know what she'd do without her.

"Sarah?" Sarah heard a knock at the door. "I don't want to scare you. It's just me." Sarah lifted her eyes from the stack of math papers she'd been grading to see Sheila standing there with a brownie in each hand. Sheila was divorced and had no children, so she often spent long hours after school in her room. "Time for a break," she called out as she plopped herself down in one of the kid's desks.

"Ah, a chocolate break. You know I can't resist chocolate," smiled Sarah. Sheila hated to see the way her friend looked. Sarah had always been vibrant, and funny.

She wore funky clothes that the kids loved, and she was many students' favorite teacher. Sheila noted the frown lines in her friend's face, the hair that was in need of a cut, and the clothes that hung on her thin frame.

"From the looks of you, you could use more than a brownie break."

"I know, I know, I need to eat more, but don't start in on me, not you. I can't take it tonight." Sheila walked over and put both brownies in front of Sarah.

"Deal; if you eat both brownies, I'll talk about whatever you want." Sarah reached for a brownie and looked at it.

"Do you know why I can't eat?" Sarah asked without expecting an answer. "Every bite of food I put into my mouth makes me wonder if Ryan starved at the bottom of some ravine. Every time I do the laundry I miss folding his clothes. The only time I can shove him to the back of my mind is when I'm teaching. And even then I can't completely throw myself into the kids."

"Nobody expects life to be the same for you Sarah. But it *can* be better than what it is now."

Sarah shook her head and wiped chocolate frosting from her mouth. "How can it get better? Each day I wake up determined to have a good day, and all it takes is one look from Ted; or Ben coming out of his bedroom and locking it, and I'll be off for the whole day."

"I know we've talked about it before, but why don't you try counseling?" offered Sheila.

"Ted won't go. He thinks it's me who's keeping the family in limbo, and Ben would never agree to it."

"Ben's only 13 years old. You're his mother, you *take* him to counseling!"

"It's not that simple. I don't even feel like I *can* be a mother to him. I've hurt him so badly by not believing that Ryan's still alive, and yet I can't believe he's completely gone either. Ted wants a memorial service. Ben would love it if we went back to the mountain to keep searching for Ryan. I truly am in limbo and I can't drag myself one way or the other."

"All the more reason you need counseling. Go without Ted. Leave Ben out of it for now. When you're stronger you can deal with them."

"You make it sound so easy Sheila. It's not that easy. What if I get counseling and I let myself believe Ryan's really dead? What do I do then? How will Ben feel? At least now he knows that I *am* in limbo, and in some twisted way I think that gives him comfort." Sarah started to pick up the second brownie but pushed it away. Sheila pushed it back in front of her.

"Hey, we had a deal. You eat both brownies and I let you talk. So eat up." Sarah remained quiet, fiddling with the wrap that had been around the brownie.

"I guess I'm all talked out," she said as she pushed the brownie back toward Sheila.

Five weeks into school and Ben still wasn't used to getting ready in the morning without Ryan. Everybody was going through the motions of being a family, but there was no heart in their actions. Ted stayed longer at the office each night and Sarah stayed in the den after dinner correcting papers. Occasionally Ben tried to talk to his parents, especially his mom. He told her he could sense Ryan, but she'd only smile and nod her head, and tell him she was happy for him. She didn't want to hear about his connections anymore because she didn't believe Ryan was coming home.

At dinner one night Ben suggested going back to the mountain that weekend, but the only answer he got from his mom was, "We've got to move on. We've got to face facts."

His dad's reaction was even stronger, "I'm never stepping foot on that mountain again, so don't bring it up to me!" Recently, his dad had been trying to talk his mom into a memorial service for Ryan. He was pushing hard but his mom was holding out for Ben to, 'come around,' which as far as Ben was concerned, wouldn't happen, if 'coming around' meant giving up on his brother. He just hoped that when Ryan finally did come home, there would be a family waiting for him.

Each night Ben checked the Internet. He surfed websites of missing kids. Nothing showed up. It was depressing seeing all the kids who were missing. He'd written the Sheriff in Mill Hollow, reminding him of his promise to ask the mountain people about Ryan when they came for winter provisions, *which should be happening soon,* he thought. Ben included another photo of Ryan just in case the flyers had been taken down. The Sheriff didn't write back.

School was a waste as far as Ben was concerned. He was used to competing with Ryan. They were excellent students and managed to support and challenge each other in academic areas as well as in sports. This year was different. Ben didn't care about school, soccer, his friends, or even his looks. He'd refused a haircut before school, knowing in his heart that Ryan's hair would be long. The thought of new clothes turned him cold.

His Dad tried to encourage him to join the soccer team but Ben refused. In his mind he didn't have time for it. Much of his time was spent lying on the bed trying to connect to Ryan, or being angry with his parents. They saw his actions as denial and depression and suggested he go to a counselor. He ignored their pleas and tuned them out. They quit bugging him. He hadn't turned on the overhead lights in his bedroom since coming home from the mountain. He left the curtains closed too. Alone, in his bedroom was the only time Ben felt even close to being whole.

Chapter 21
October 19

Ted and Sarah cleared away the dinner dishes in silence. Ben had already slammed and locked the door to his bedroom for the night and was playing loud music. Tonight was the first time all three had been together for dinner in over a week and Sarah tried to make it a festive meal with Ted's favorite stuffed pork chops and chocolate pie for Ben. Other than the food, nothing was very festive. The conversation, when it happened was stilted. There were silences that dragged on too long. Someone, usually Sarah, broke it with a bit of news from school or a question, but her voice sounded flat and hollow even to her.

Ben was sullen and refused dessert. Tears welled behind Sarah's eyes, but she blinked them away. They had to get over this, or at least get beyond it. The three of them needed to become a family again. She took another step toward what she hoped would help accomplish this while she and Ted were filling the dishwasher.

"It's nice to have you here for dinner."

"You know I'm working on a big account. I can't be home for dinner every night! The partners carried me long enough. I need to pull my weight now." He slammed water glasses onto the top shelf while he was talking. As if to emphasize his angry words the last glass broke and a shard punctured his palm. He pulled his hand away and walked over to the sink. Sarah's heart fell. She wondered if she should go to him or let him work out his own frustrations. In the past, before Ryan's disappearance, she wouldn't have hesitated to offer help. Unfortunately, nothing about life was that simple anymore. She decided to act as if things were fine and see where it led.

Slowly she put her arms around Ted's waist while he let cool water run over his hand. "It's just that I miss you. I'm not complaining. I know you're doing your best, but Ben misses you too." She squeezed a little harder and went on, "His math teacher stopped me in the hall today to tell me he's eight assignments behind. In math, for goodness sake, that's his best subject. I'm afraid to ask how he's doing in his other classes."

Ted's back stiffened as he turned the water off and grabbed for paper towel to wrap around his hand. "You're afraid of a lot these days, aren't you? Afraid to admit that one son is gone, and the other one is falling apart. Afraid to hold a memorial service to give this whole thing some closure, and afraid to…what difference does it make anymore? I give up." Sarah dropped her hands and backed away letting him go to the medicine cabinet alone.

How dare he talk to me like that, Sarah thought. *I've been holding things together at work and at home. What's he been doing to hold up his end?* She slammed the dishwasher closed leaving the broken glass inside, flicked off the light and headed back to school to correct the day's work.

The Burns' family continued to drift apart, splintering like four compass points. The only one who could gather them back together was 500 miles away, and about to meet the first neighbor since he'd been with the Riley's.

Chapter 22
October 19

Amos took Ryan to a different part of the mountain today. He'd gotten used to riding on Nearly behind Amos and the fall scenery was beautiful. Amos wasn't one to talk much so Ryan had the quiet to himself. He snuck a look at his watch 11:20 a.m. Ben would be going to lunch soon, if this was a weekday. There was no way of telling one day from the next in the mountains. There wasn't a school or a church that Ryan knew about. Nearly stopped and Amos got off. After tying Nearly to a tree he walked a few yards away. Ryan stayed on the horse waiting for instructions. He never knew what Amos might want him to do and he'd learned the hard way not to guess what it might be.

"Git down here, Charlie," ordered Amos. He'd left his rifle in the saddle so Ryan did the same and slid off the horse. He tried to learn by watching. Today his curiosity was aroused. Amos was ahead of Ryan by about 12 feet. He was scanning the ground so Ryan did the same.

"What are we looking for Pa?" The name still stuck in his throat, but the consequences of not calling him Pa, hurt worse. He didn't think his nose would look the same, not that he'd been able to look at it since there were no mirrors in the house.

"Our traps boy. What did ye figger we was lookin' fer in this part a the woods? This is our trappin' fields."

Ryan froze, *traps,* he thought. His mind went immediately to pictures he'd seen on the Animal Channel that he and Ben watched. He knew traps could be a cruel way for an animal to die. Some gnawed through their leg to get away and others like the coyote, brought the mate food while it was trapped and waited until he or she died.

"Come on, keep goin' Charlie!" Amos's harsh words started Ryan's feet again. "We got a dozen traps here's 'bout ta check." Ryan feared the worst and imagined his own foot getting trapped so he stepped even more carefully.

Up ahead he saw Amos squat down. *Oh God, Oh God,* prayed Ryan, *Let it be empty!* He approached slowly, hearing Amos struggle with something metal.

"Come on, boy, gimme a hand. We got us a fox!" Ryan stopped just behind Amos. He wasn't sure he'd ever seen anything this awful before. The fox was covered with blood from about his left hindquarter down. The leg was nearly chopped off and the fox was lifeless and limp. "Take him back ta Nearly and bring the water. We'll wash the trap and set it agin." Ryan didn't move. Amos turned around, still squatting beside the fox. He saw the boy's pale face and wondered if maybe Ma was right about the boy. He still wasn't right in the head and didn't remember a lot of what he'd been taught.

"Come on Charlie. He won't bite ye. He ain't got no more bite left. See?" Amos picked up the fox and broke off the rest of the leg and threw it into the bushes. Ryan bent over and threw up. Amos shook his head and walked the fox back to Nearly and thrust the water at Ryan when he returned.

"Here, take a drink. How ye gonna be able ta fend fer yerself and a wife up here in the hills if ye don't trap? It's 'bout time ta take the hides ta town. How do ye think we'd git by without these traps?"

When Amos was done with his short speech Ryan realized this was about as gentle as he'd seen him. Still, something snapped inside of Ryan, something that had been building ever since the day he first walked to the privy by himself. He started quietly but his voice rose. "I don't want to trap. I don't want to live in the mountains! I don't want a wife! Can't you see I'm not Charlie? Are you really that dumb?" Ryan had been looking down screaming these words into the ground so he didn't see Amos approaching until he felt the blow to his cheek."

"I told ye boy. No more talk like that!" Ryan's head reeled from the force of Amos's swat but this time he stood his ground, and didn't fall. Ryan held back his tears, took a long look at Amos and then walked back to Nearly.

Ryan laid his head on Nearly's flank and cried. He could feel his face begin to swell and knew he'd have another bruise in the morning. He had to get away and he'd just blown all his intentions to butter Amos up so he would take him to town. He lifted his head and walked to the nearest tree, careful that he didn't step on a trap. He let his thoughts wander as he held his cheek with one hand and poked at his teeth with the other. Nothing seemed loose. *This is the last time Amos is going to hit me.* He vowed. *I'm getting out of here even if I don't know where I'm going. It can't be any worse than this.* He revised his latest escape plan. Instead of going to town with Amos he'd wait until Amos went to town, then he'd gather a few supplies and leave. Ryan knew Lizzie Sue couldn't stop him and he didn't really think she'd try. But that was still weeks away. He laid his head on his arms and cried like he hadn't cried since he was a baby.

As often happens after someone is cried out, Ryan fell asleep. He wasn't sure how long he'd been sleeping when he heard Amos come back. He felt stiff and a little disoriented. He remembered crying and then his mind worked backwards to the slap, his screaming at Amos, puking in the bushes, watching Amos break the leg off the fox. He stood up, keeping his back to the tree and looked at Amos with as much bravery as he could muster. He wiped the dirt and tears from his face and saw what Amos was carrying.

He had three more foxes and a handful of rabbits. His good fortune seemed to erase any lingering anger. "Look here Charlie, we got a haul taday!' Ryan mounted Nearly without a word, and waited for Amos to strap the dead animals to the horse and get on himself. The ride back to the cabin was even quieter than the ride out had been. Ryan's mind was filled with nothing but thoughts of escape, and hate for the man riding in front of him. He took great care not to touch him.

Chapter 23
October 19

Lizzie Sue heard the horse long before she saw Jack. Pa and the boy were out checking traps but she knew Jack McKay wouldn't leave before he'd sat a while with Pa. It was over half a day's hard ride to the McKay's place, and the trip wasn't taken lightly.

Lizzie Sue was waiting outside when Jack rode up. "Howdy, Jack. What brings ye here?" Her heart was pounding, knowing that Pa and the boy could come home any time.

"Howdy, Miz Lizzie," said Jack tipping the brim of his leather hat and getting off his horse. Jack was about the same age as Pa, somewhere in his early fifties. He was as round as Pa was tall, but could still move like a man half his age if he had a mind to move at all. He was a lazy man with red hair like Lizzie Sue's and piercing green eyes. Snake eyes, Lizzie Sue thought every time she saw him. He also had the yellowest teeth she'd ever seen. All of his features taken together made him a hard man to look at.

"I'm goin' ta Mill Hollow tamorrow, Miz Lizzie, and I wondered if ye and Amos needed anythin' afore his trip."

"Ain't ye a little early this year, Jack?"

"Yeah, Becca's bout to have her baby and I cain't leave her alone in another month." Becca was Jack's second wife. He'd buried Ellie his first wife, 15 years ago. Lizzie Sue knew that even though Becca was plenty old enough to birth a baby she was scared. Lizzie Sue didn't blame her. The mountains were a hard place to raise an infant. Ellie's babies never made it to a year and she'd died during the last birth even though Lizzie Sue had been there to help her through it.

Lizzie Sue was shaking on the inside thinking of Ryan, but she managed to say, "Amos'll be here soon. Kin I git ye some coffee and cobbler?"

"Might neighborly of ye Miz Lizzie." After Lizzie Sue served Jack a plate of apple cobbler they visited for an hour. All the while Lizzie Sue was only half listening, fretting about the boy, twirling her fingers in her apron, wondering what Jack would say when he saw him? Funerals, hardship, weddings and births were generally the only reasons neighbors got together on this part of the mountain, and Jack had come to Charlie's burial.

Chapter 24
October 19

Visiting with Jack wasn't easy for Lizzie Sue even on happy occasions, and this didn't qualify as one of those. She was sure Jack noticed her jumping up to look out the window every time she heard a noise. She had no idea what to do. Part of her wanted to let Jack see the boy and end this nightmare. The other part of her felt she had to protect Amos and his refound happiness...and if she was honest with herself...her love of the boy too.

Something snapped outside and Lizzie Sue flew to the window. She was staring so hard that the sound of Jack's voice right behind her made her jump. "What're ye lookin' fer, Miz Lizzie? Ye're more skittery'n a newborn colt!" Lizzie Sue turned back to face Jack. She was sure he could see her heart pounding like a summer storm on the tin roof.

Lizzie Sue turned around and eased her way past Jack's bulk. "Jist missin' my man," she offered as she sat back at the table, heart still hammering in her chest.

Ryan continued to concentrate on the land around him. His head hurt from his emotional outburst, from the sun overhead, from Amos's slap, and from trying so hard to see a way off this mountain prison. He was hungry and the swelling around his mouth ached. He wondered again if he had a loose tooth. Keeping his eyes sharp he thought, *Something has to look familiar! Something's got to help me get out of here. I can't take it much longer!*

Just then an eagle screeched overhead. Ryan's heart jumped in his chest. *Could this be one of the eagles from the aerie dad wanted to find? If it is, and I can find the aerie, I should be able to look down and see Mill Hollow below.* Ryan twisted around trying to keep the eagle in sight.

"What're ye doin' back there? Sit still! Nearly's got herself a load. She don't need ye bouncin' round."

"It's the eagle...Pa." Ryan began, knowing that Amos always softened a bit when he called him Pa. "Where does it nest? Is it somewhere around here?" Ryan's heart was pounding and his breath was coming in short gasps. *Could it really be this easy? Just asking Amos and finding the nest?*

"Ye know where they are. We bin there lots a times." Amos chuckled, "When ye was jist a youngen ye wanted ta climb down and play with the little houses ye saw down in Mill Hollow. That's why I whittled ye them little houses ta play with, the ones Ma keeps on the window by the sink."

Ryan's heart stopped. *It was the right aerie!* He took a risk and said, "Let's go Pa! It can't be that far. I want to see it again."

"Ma's waitin' fer us. We got no time fer goin' off'n that way what with you not helpin' with the traps."

Ryan took a deep breath. "I'm sorry Pa. I'll do better next time. It won't take long. Please can we go? Please?"

Amos didn't say a word. He pulled on Nearly and turned off the slightly worn path. Ryan took note of everything. He wasn't sure, but he thought they'd turned east. His eyes scanned the area frantically, looking for anything that could serve as a landmark. He saw trees, rocks and dirt, grass, dead flowers, weeds. There was nothing different about this area than any of the other areas he'd seen

134

on the mountain. His head was beginning to hurt worse from the strain of trying to memorize the landscape. Nearly moved too slowly for Ryan but he reminded himself to sit still. He didn't want to upset Amos again. His excitement was barely contained when he spotted a huge outcropping of rock. It was larger at the bottom than at the top, with a smaller, cinched-in part in the middle. It looked like the rock had been whittled away where a belt would be. And then it hit Ryan. *It looks like a snowman! I can find this place again. I know I can!*

A few minutes later the dense trees opened to a meadow with fewer tall trees. The eagle was back in sight and Ryan could no more control his excitement than Nearly could have sprouted wings to fly. The lifeless wildflowers and tall grasses gave way to more and more flat, grey rock. Suddenly Amos reined-in Nearly and she stopped. Ryan jumped off before Amos could say a word.

He ran to the edge and looked up to see the nests. They weren't hard to find because they were so huge. There were three of them, spaced many trees apart. It was an awesome sight and Ryan couldn't help think of his family. *Had they found this spot? Had they looked up and seen these same nests?* But more importantly *Had they been this close to me?* Then he squatted, crawled to the edge, and looked down to see the small town. It was tinier and farther away than he thought it would be, but it was there-Mill Hollow!

"Kinda looks like a doll's village don't it?"

Ryan willed his body to stay in control. He wanted to start down right now. *Just do it!* His body was telling him. *Get away from Amos. Go over the edge and get away before he knows what happened to him.* But the rational part of him commanded his body to stop shaking and get rid of those crazy thoughts. Even so, he couldn't take his eyes off the town below because there, he knew, lay his freedom and the way back to his family. *I won't blow it now, not when I'm so close to getting away. I'll watch how to get back, grab some provisions, and maybe I can get away tomorrow!* Tomorrow, it had such a nice ring to it. *I need to pay really close attention to how we get back to the cabin so I can retrace the steps tomorrow.*

"Are ye happy now?" asked Amos.

"Oh yes, Pa!" breathed Ryan.

"Then let's git."

Lizzie and Jack were back at the table. She'd listened to Jack talk about every little ache and pain in his big, bloated body until she finally got up to fetch her medicine bag. Boiling water, steeping herbs and serving Jack tea took her mind off Amos's return for a while; at least until she heard a horse. She knew it had to be Nearly. She could tell by the sun they were overdue, and she hadn't started dinner, which was the least of her worries. "Amos back?" asked Jack craning his neck toward the window.

"Seems like it, don't it?" breathed Lizzie Sue. "Ye stay where ye be and let the tea do its work. I'll go see ta Nearly and git Amos in ta see ye." Lizzie Sue made herself slow down and walk to the door, but once it banged behind her she ran toward Amos.

"Pa! Pa!" She was using her apron to wave him away from the house.

"What is it, Ma? Are ye okay?"

"Jack's inside Pa!"

"What's Jack doin' here?"

"He's goin' ta town early 'cause Becca's 'bout ta birth her youngen. He wants ta know if we kin use anythin' afore you go."

"Well then, let's git inside Charlie. Jack'll be happy ta see ye!"

Ryan froze. He sensed what happened next would be very important to his escape. He could see that Lizzie Sue was acting strangely. He wasn't sure if he should run into the house and scream for help, or if he should hide. Lizzie Sue took the decision out of his hands. "No, the boy needs ta see ta somethin' in the shed with me." She jerked Ryan's sleeve as if to pull him bodily from the horse. Ryan slid off Nearly. Amos dismounted and started for the house. Lizzie Sue grabbed Nearly's reins and headed to the small barn. Ryan glanced over his shoulder toward the house and spotted the huge, hairy face of a man in the cabin window. The way the man looked made Ryan think it was better to go with Lizzie Sue.

She yanked him around and Ryan was surprised by how strong she was. "Don't let him see ye! No good'll come ta anythin' from that man."

Amos barged into his house. Jack's greeting was, "Who is that boy? He looks a might like Charlie."

"It is Charlie. Who do ye think it is? He's come back. Kin ye believe it?"

"Have ye gone soft in the haid Amos? What do ye mean Charlie's come back? I seed him put in the ground more'n a year ago now. He's up on that hill." Jack jerked his thumb behind him, pointing toward the hill with the pine cross.

Jack's comment was lost on Amos. He ignored it and went on, "Ye saw him fer yerself Jack. It's Charlie. Sit fer awhile. He'll be surprised ta see ye. Ma needed him ta tend ta somethin' in the shed. She was in some kinda hurry."

Jack sat back down, not caring anymore if he got home past midnight. He wasn't leaving until he saw that boy, whoever he was. Just then Lizzie Sue came in wringing her hands on her apron, and slightly out of breath. "Where's Charlie Ma? Jack wants ta see him fer himself."

"I'm sure he'd like ta see Charlie, Pa, but that ain't gonna happen." Jack stared open-mouthed while Lizzie Sue continued. "I sent him off ta pick some herbs I been needin'. Ye kept him out so long taday that he didn't git his other chores done. These'r special herbs I'm gonna need when Becca's baby's borned." She was still breathing heavily and Jack noticed that her eyes kept darting toward the window. Jack's face fell. There was no way he could wait until the boy got done herb picking. Besides when Lizzie Sue mentioned Becca he knew she'd be getting worried about now, so he finished up his business with Amos and accepted a bag of herbs from Lizzie Sue to use for his aches and pains. Jack had plenty to keep his mind occupied on the trip back to his wife.

Chapter 25
October 19

Ted stopped the car at the mailbox and looked inside. If mail was there it meant Sarah was at work and wouldn't be home for dinner again. He reached for the mail and threw it on the seat beside him.

"Ben!" he called, entering the mudroom from the attached garage. "Ben, are you here?" Ted walked through the kitchen and to the bottom of the stairs leading up to the second floor. "Ben, get down here if you're home!" He returned to the kitchen and started to throw the mail into the drawer referred to as the 'holding tank' but something caught his eye. It stood out because the address was hand-written and was addressed to Ben. The return envelope was postmarked Heywood, Virginia. Ted knew that Heywood was the closest large city to Mill Hollow. He held the letter up to the light. It looked like a single sheet of paper folded over. He tapped it on the edge of the table to settle the paper into the envelope and tore one end off. What he read from the sheriff in Mill Hollow angered him.

Dear Ben,

I'm sorry to report that I haven't yet seen any trappers from the mountains coming for their winter provisions. It's still early for them to be here, but I promise you that when they do come down I won't forget our agreement to show each one Ryan's picture and ask if they've seen him.

Thank you for the photo of Ryan, it's much clearer than the picture on the 'Child Missing' posters. I'm sorry that you're having a hard time with your parents right now. I think that would be expected after all you've gone through.

I'll write again when the mountain people start coming to town, or, you can e-mail me anytime. And don't worry, you're not bothering me. Good luck at home.

Sincerely,
John Martin, Sheriff
Mill Hollow, VA

Ted put the letter back into the envelope and left it on the kitchen table. He went to his room to change into sweats and go for a run. He needed to work off some tension.

It was 6:45 p.m. when Ben got home. No lights were on in the house even though his dad's car was in the garage. Things as usual, he figured with his dad out running and his mom at school. He'd spent the hours after school walking around town. He had no destination in mind but soon found himself at the video arcade. He spent most of his allowance losing himself in kickboxing figures on the gaming screen. His hand was sore from hitting the side of the game when he messed up. One of the losers who worked there came over and told him he'd have to leave if he didn't stop hitting the machine. The guy was no older than 16 or 17, and only about as tall as Ben. Ben gave him a look that said, *If you know what's good for you you'll get out of my face!* And that's just

140

what the kid did. Ben had been perfecting this angry rebel look for weeks – it kept a lot of people off his case and out of his business.

On the way home Ben's mind found its way to Ryan. His thoughts were jumbled, only half formed as they came out. He saw Ryan laughing, and then he saw Ryan scared of something, but as soon as that image came he saw Ryan laying in a small room, and then Ryan was crying. Ben shook his head. None of his connections were clear lately and it scared him. *Is Ryan in danger? Is he really dead and I just can't accept it?* As soon as that thought entered his head he pushed it aside. *I'd know if he was dead. I need to concentrate to get clearer feelings.* He ran the rest of the way home.

When he got there and found no one home he was almost happy: no confrontations, no questions, just him alone in his bedroom with his thoughts and his music. When he flipped the light he noticed the envelope in the center of the kitchen table. He turned it over and saw it was addressed to him, and had been opened. "I can't even open my own mail around here!" he shouted to the empty house. He stomped up the stairs, unlocked his bedroom door and flopped on his bed.

Chapter 26
October 19

    The tin bucket Lizzie Sue gave Ryan was almost full of late season seedpods. It was a special herb Lizzie Sue taught him to recognize. Ryan didn't realize he'd been methodically filling up the bucket. His mind was trying to sort out all that had happened today. Finding the eagle's aerie and Mill Hollow below, changed everything. He'd set landmarks in his mind and was sure he could find his way back. Then, he'd seen the stranger at the house, and had no idea what this new twist could, or could not mean for him. *Would the neighbor just accept that Lizzie Sue and Amos' son had somehow come back from the dead? And if he's willing to accept that, then he'd be just as crazy as Amos. But if the neighbor didn't believe it, then he might send someone to help.* Ryan wondered if he should go back and see what's happening, or take off from where he was right now. He looked at the sun, which was going down around him, creating orange hues through the sparse mountain pines.

    Ryan decided to wait another day before his escape. That would mean he could get provisions to help him beat the odds of making it to Mill Hollow. He would also be able to travel in the daylight. Ryan's next thought surprised him; *I've got to consider Ma too.*

    She'd carved a place in Ryan's heart as sure as CRLE was carved in the pine cross on the hill marking Charlie's grave. *I can't hurt her by walking away without saying good-bye. It'd be like she was losing Charlie all over again.* Ryan thought about how Lizzie Sue had nursed him back to health, hovered around him, tried to protect him from Amos, stitched his wounds, cooked for him, and talked with him. He never would have made it without her, and he knew he owed it to her, and to himself, to say good-bye.

Ryan shoved the pods further into the bucket and absently looked around. He'd miss how this quiet seeped into his soul. As bad as this nightmare had been he *had* survived and he'd learned how to do it without his mom or dad or his twin. It was then he knew he'd gotten as much from these hills as they'd taken away from him. He'd call it even, as long as he got home safely. He didn't want anything bad to happen to Amos and Lizzie Sue. He just wanted to get away and start his life again with his real family.

Jack rode his old grey horse as hard as he dared before the trail was lost to the darkness. He wasn't worried about losing his way since he'd lived his whole life in the mountains, but he didn't want his horse hurting her leg by stepping in a hole. He had news to give Becca, news so strange that it might take her mind off the coming baby. He couldn't wait to share it with her.

Jack began shouting for Becca before he got off his horse. She came running out the door, holding her big belly. She followed Jack to the lean-to where he took care of his horse and told her about the boy at Amos's house. "How kin that be Jack? We was both at Charlie's burial."

"I don't know Becca, but the kid I saw was a sure match fer Charlie, and Amos called him Charlie."

"What did Lizzie Sue have to say?" asked Becca.

"She was nervous as a chicken facin' a farmer with a axe. She sent the boy out ta get some herbs or some such thin' as soon's as he got back with Amos." Becca shook her head and waited for Jack to say more. "I know'd I went a little crazy when Ellie died, but this thin' with Amos seems worse'n that," responded Jack. "I never believed Ellie was anyplace but in her grave. I don't think Amos believes Charlie's really dead and buried."

"There's some folks around here still says ye're a might tetched in the haid," teased Becca. Jack laughed with his wife and they walked hand in hand to their cabin. Once inside Becca flopped in her rocking chair and Jack in his.

"Who do ye think that boy kin be, Jack?" This *was* just the sort of news Becca needed to take her mind off the coming labor pains. She was tall and skinny, everywhere that is, except her belly. People on the mountain thought because Rebecca was such a big girl she wouldn't fear things. But a secret only Jack knew, was that Becca was scared of lots of things; snakes, lightning, creaks in the night, and most of all, having this baby. She wanted the baby as much as she'd wanted anything in her life, but she wanted it to be over. Jack teased her about her fears and made them seem smaller. This made Becca enjoy life with him.

Becca wore her hair pulled back and braided. It came halfway down her back, and swung back and forth when she walked. Jack liked to tell her that her face and arms had more freckles than the sky had stars. She had on one of Jack's denim shirts and a pair of his pants with the legs rolled up. There was no need for maternity clothes in the mountains, and no money for them either.

"I don't know who that boy is," answered Jack, "but I aim ta find out 'bout him soon's I git ta town. Amos acted like everythin' was jist fine. But Lizzie Sue didn't. Somethin's not right, and when I git ta town I aim ta poke 'round a bit."

"Ye think ye should take this piece a gossip off a the mountain?" Becca enjoyed the distraction, but like most of the mountain people, she enjoyed the privacy the mountain afforded. "I don't want ye bringin' no trouble ta the mountain jist as my birthin' time's here." She rubbed her swollen belly in small gentle circles.

"I'll sleep on it Becky and maybe there'll be an answer in my dreams." Becca got up to pack a meal for Jack on his trip to town. Jack got busy finishing the wooden crib he was making for his baby.

All through supper Lizzie Sue watched Ryan and sensed that something had changed about him. He had the same kind of look that would have made her own mama say, "Ye look like a cat that's jist swallowed a bird." She knew he'd seen Jack through the window, and she knew Jack had seen the boy. She wondered what would come of this encounter, and it worried her. But, aside from the obvious she still thought the boy was acting strangely. He was holding his shoulders a little straighter, and he ate with more appetite, and smiled at her when their eyes met. Lizzie Sue knew these things weren't anything big on their own, just things a mother would notice about her son. If she was pushed to put a name to it she'd say that Ryan seemed happier. Thinking about his happiness made her feel a little sadder. *I've got a mess a feelin's ta sort out tonight while Pa's doin' his whittlin' and Ryan's in the loft.*

Amos' booming voice broke the silence. "Tell yer Ma where's ye got me ta take ye, Charlie."

Ryan swallowed his food before starting to talk. Something, he noticed, Amos never did. "Pa took me to see the eagle's nesting place. You know the one Ma? The one I always loved when I was little?"

Lizzie Sue answered, "I ain't seed that spot since I were a youngen and I near fergot about it. Tell me 'bout it." But she didn't listen to what was said after that. *So that's it,* she thought, *he's seed the town and knows how ta git away.* She looked at Amos and her heart ached for him; she looked at Ryan and her heart ached for him too. She had no time for the ache in her own heart. Then it came to her, like it was sent from above, or maybe from Charlie. She knew what she had to do, and when she had it done, she could tend to the biggest heartache - hers.

Chapter 27
October 20

Becca wrapped the morning's leftover cornbread in paper and stuffed it in her husband's pack with the rest of the food he'd be taking. "Did yer dream tell ye what ta do 'bout the boy, Jack?"

"I think it did Becca. I need ta do some sniffin' 'round when I'm in Mill Hollow. If'n this boy's missin' there'll be some sign or somethin'. Then Becca, I won't be bringin' no trouble ta the mountain, cuz it's already here." He gave his wife a hug and went out the door.

Becca sat in the rocker with her hands on her belly and started dreaming about what it would feel like to have your baby taken from you. She couldn't imagine Lizzie Sue going along with anything like that. Lizzie Sue loved Charlie too much to inflict that meanness on another woman. Becca had known Lizzie Sue all her life and Lizzie Sue was the closest thing she had to a friend. She knew Lizzie Sue would be there for her when the baby's time came. *I wish I could go see Lizzie Sue right now,* Becca thought, *I could see the boy fer myself and I could git Lizzie ta talk ta me.*

Ben looked at himself in the bathroom mirror and liked what he saw. His hair reached almost to his shoulders and he had a gold earring hanging from his left ear. He smiled at his dad freaking out over a little hole in his ear. *Dad noticed me that night!* He pulled at a hole in his jeans, to make it bigger. He sat on his bed to put on his black leather boots.

When Sarah took Ben school shopping she'd balked at the idea of getting him black boots, instead of tennis shoes. In the end he'd worn her down and decided to let him find his own way through his identity crisis over losing his brother.

Ben stood up and pulled a wrinkled black tee shirt over his head and then topped it off with a black leather vest he'd bought without his parent's permission. "Smokin!" he said aloud to the image of himself. He closed and locked his bedroom door and headed downstairs for the first of many confrontations he'd have with his parents today. He looked forward to it.

Chapter 28
October 20

"Boy, git down here." Lizzie Sue was standing on the bottom rung of the ladder to the loft. Ryan looked at his watch; it said 9:38. They'd let him sleep in for some reason. He rubbed his eyes. "Boy, do ye hear me?" Ryan remembered today was the day he was leaving. How could he still be sleeping?

"I'm coming." Ryan slipped on jeans and a shirt, bringing his socks and shoes down the ladder with him. He looked around and saw no sign of Amos. Next he looked on the hooks above the door where the guns were kept, and one was missing. "Where's Amos?" Ryan asked. He never called him Pa when he was gone.

"He's gone fer now, that's all ye need to know. Come on, we ain't got all day if ye're goin' ta Mill Hollow afore dark."

Ryan couldn't believe his ears. "What do you mean?"

"I know'd that's what's on yer mind ever since ye told me 'bout the eagle's nest."

"How?" asked Ryan.

"I got a kinda special sense 'bout folks I'm close ta," she answered.

"Does that mean you feel close to me?" Ryan's hands were shaky and his heart thudded.

"Well I must, or I wouldn't a know'd yer thoughts now would I? And I wouldn't a convinced Pa to git me some special willow bark which is the opposite way of where you'll be headin'."

Ryan began to smile. "Lizzie Sue, you're helping me get away?"

"I reckon I am. It come ta me last night like a flash from above. I need ta help ye git away. I ain't thought what ta tell Pa, though. His heart's goin' ta split in two this time. I don't know if he kin take losin' his boy two times. I don't think his mind kin take it agin." She wiped a tear away from her cheek.

"You know I can't stay here, don't you Lizzie Sue?"

"I wouldn't be riskin' my man's mind if'n I didn't think I was doin' the right thin'. But it don't make it any easier, do it?" She looked at the boy who she had grown to love and stifled a sob. *There'll be enough time fer cryin' later.*

"No it doesn't make it any easier." He crossed the few steps to wrap the tiny woman in his arms. "Thanks Ma," he whispered.

She clutched at the boy who looked so much like Charlie and said, "Come on Ryan, we got work ta do." For the next few minutes Lizzie Sue wrapped cornbread, cold rabbit stew, and cobbler in the precious newspaper that Amos brought from town once a year. She put it all into the tin pail and topped it off with a canning jar of water. Then she got Charlie's gun, loaded it and handed it to Ryan. She stuck some extra shotgun shells in his pocket. "Take these things," Lizzie Sue was pointing to the pail. "I wish't it were more, but it'll have ta do. Now, kin ye remember how ta git ta the nestin' place? I ain't bin there since I was a youngen myself."

"I know I can get there again," said Ryan.

"Then ye best be gittin'."

"I'll take the food and water but I don't want the gun."

"Take it Ryan. I'll feel better knowin' ye have it." Ryan nodded his head as he looked at this Lizzie Sue and knew he'd miss her ways. "I could have left last night when I was seedpod picking."

"What kept ye then, the darkness?"

"That was part of it," Ryan answered truthfully, "but it was also because I couldn't leave without saying good bye to you." The tears, which had been threatening to fall all morning finally spilled over onto her face. She didn't wipe them away. Ryan felt like crying too, and he wasn't sure why; *this should be the happiest day of my life.* He was going home to his family and school, soccer and ice cream and all the other things he'd missed. He hugged Lizzie Sue once more and said, "Good bye. I wouldn't have made it without you. I won't forget you."

"Go on now," she said pushing Ryan away from her and giving him a shove toward the door. "I let ye sleep some this mornin' cuz you'll be needin' all yer strength and more. Be careful Ryan!" He picked up the berry pail and hoisted the gun over his shoulder, took one last look at the tiny cabin that had been both a source of healing and hurting for him, looked again at Lizzie Sue and headed out the door.

Lizzie Sue watched Ryan walk away until she couldn't see him anymore. Then she grabbed the hoe and went out to get her garden ready for the winter.

151

Chapter 29
October 20

Ben's choice of school clothes started his parent's morning off wrong. *Serves them right. They deserve this and a whole lot more for bailing on Ryan. 'Ryan,' the name still sent a wave of grief through him.* It had been a while since he'd felt a connection with his brother. He couldn't bear the thought of losing this thin thread of hope and hadn't told anyone about losing it.. He could barely even let *himself* think about it. The more he rebelled against his parents and school, the weaker the link with his twin got. The more tenuous his invisible lifeline became, the more he felt like rebelling. It was a vicious cycle. He thought he'd blow a gasket if his mom asked him one more time about a memorial service for Ryan.

It was bad enough enduring the neighbors and friends bringing over casseroles and condolences when they first got home. Each time he silently accepted their words of comfort or ate a mouthful of tuna casserole from one of them, he felt like he was letting Ryan down. All he wanted to do was scream for them to go home because Ryan was alive! *Connection or no connection I'll never believe he's dead!*

Riding to school with his mom every morning was barely tolerable. She tried to talk to him about school, the weather, or dinner that night, but those chit-chatty things sounded so lame he barely listened. He thought it was pitiful how her eyes never settled on his face. She must have known they fell on deaf ears.

Ben smiled to himself as he looked in the visor mirror and checked his hair. It was now long enough to pull back into a ponytail. He hadn't tried it yet. Right now he liked the way his hair could hide part of his face and he only had to look at the world with one eye. He knew his hair and choice of clothing were driving his parents crazy, but as far as he was concerned he was just winding up. He'd skipped school twice just to wander around town and was planning on skipping again today. When his mom dropped him off he acted like he was going in but as soon as she drove off to the faculty lot he turned and walked away. It was so easy!

He didn't want his teachers telling his mom – so he hadn't skipped much – but school was lame. It held nothing except sad memories of what this year was meant to be. He was supposed to be walking into school with Ryan, hitting each other playfully, racing to their lockers. They were supposed to be challenging each other in class, seeing who could get the highest marks on quizzes. It was *NOT* supposed to be like this! There were times, like today, where he just couldn't take it anymore; no more sad looks from teachers, no more *'understanding'* no matter what kind of crap he handed in on his papers; and no more passing kids in the hall who had just gotten word of the sad story, and nudged each other, pointing with their chins like he couldn't see them.

He never knew what might start things off wrong, but something always did. It could be as benign as passing an empty locker, or seeing Mrs. Freeman, the teacher they hoped to get for social studies, and suddenly the whole school would close in on him and he'd feel hot and sick to his stomach. Deep down he knew he should go to a counselor like his mom and dad wanted, but that seemed like giving up. *Hang in there, get through each day as best I can and soon everyone'll see I'm right.*

The first time he skipped school he met some kids at the arcade. They liked him right away. He might not have looked twice at them if Ryan had been with him, but this year was different. They didn't know he had a twin and they knew nothing about his life so he could be whoever he wanted to be around them. The second time he met up with them he had gotten his ear pierced. One of them had dared him, and he'd let the guy do it with a hot safety pin. John let Ben use one of his spare earrings until he could get one of his own. It hurt when they poked the safety pin through his earlobe but he didn't let them see it. He knew they were waiting for him to cry or scream, but when he didn't it was like he'd passed some sort of initiation rite, and they were all over him high-fiven' and patting him on the back like he was now some desperate member of an elite social circle. *Whatever!*

He couldn't face school today. He was tired of everyone not mentioning Ryan's name even though it hung between them like a pig on a barbecue spit, sizzling and popping just under the surface.

Chapter 30
October 20, 10:48 a.m.

The metal pail handle was slicing through Ryan's fingers. Every few steps he switched the pail from hand to hand, which meant he also had to switch the hand that held the gun. *Why'd I agree to take this thing? It's not like I'm going to shoot it. I'm done with shooting guns. I don't want to see another gun as long as I live.* The sound of the wildcat he'd narrowly escaped when he'd been lost popped into his mind and he had second thoughts. He stopped and set both the pail and the gun down, took out the glass jar, unscrewed the lid, and drank greedily. He knew the more he drank, the lighter his pail would get but he also remembered his terrible thirst of months ago when he was wandering around the mountains lost and scared. He resisted taking another drink and screwed the lid back on. He was a wiser boy today than he'd been that summer morning following the eagle.

As Ryan walked, thoughts jumped from one thing to another like a hummingbird darting in and out of a flower. First he thought of Lizzie Sue and how the gun, pail and glass jar wouldn't be easy to replace. Then he thought about his mom and wondered what she was doing. As fast as she came into his mind, he'd think of Ben at school. Then for no reason McDonald's popped into his mind and the thought of a Big Mac made his mouth water. Finally, he remembered where he was and what he was doing and he'd look around for signs of dangers, and on, and on, and on, until it was time to switch hands or rest again.

After another hour of walking he pulled out the cold stew and cornbread. It hit him that Lizzie Sue would never know if her food helped him get home. *Home!* It sounded so good. He licked the last of the cold stew from the paper, rubbed his sore hands together, picked up the bucket and gun, and headed toward where he hoped was the snowman rock.

The day grew grey and overcast. When the sun did shine, it cut the gold and red of the leaves like a knife through warm butter. This time Ryan took notice of the mountain. He was determined to be smarter. He remembered how easy it was to lose your footing on the loose rock. Taking one careful step at a time brought him that much closer to his family.

Lizzie Sue still wasn't sure what she was going to tell Pa. She'd worked all morning thinking of nothing else. Now that she saw her husband approaching, her mind was blank and her body shaking. *I did the right thing but Pa won't see it that way. Has Ryan gotten far enough away?*

Amos opened the door and set the willow bark on the table. "Where's Charlie, Ma? We got time ta check the traps afore dinner." Amos stepped on the lowest rung of the loft ladder. He stuck his head over the flooring and saw the straw bed rolled up and the night pot gone. The nightshirt peg was empty too. Amos stepped down and looked at Ma. She stepped forward and took her husband's rough hands in hers.

"Amos, Charlie's gone."

"Gone where, Ma?"

"He's gone ta heaven, Pa." Lizzie Sue's voice was trembling.

"No, Ma. We thought he'd gone ta heaven but he come back ta us. He's here somewhere's." Amos jerked his head around wildly. His eyes darting everywhere, not focusing on anything for more than a split second, looking for any sign that the boy was still there.

"Pa, that weren't Charlie ye brought back here half daid. Charlie's up on the hill. Remember, ye carved his name on the fancy cross ye made?" Amos shook his head, looking down at Lizzie Sue. "We had a nice rememberin' service fer him. Jack and Becca was here, and so was Tilly, Mae, Henry and lotsa others." Lizzie Sue was losing control of her voice. "Come on, Pa. We'll go see Charlie." She led Amos outside and toward the cross on the hill. Amos allowed his wife to keep his hand and steer him up the hill as if he were a small child.

At the family cemetery Amos was confused and wasn't sure why Ma wanted to show him this cross. He vaguely recognized it as something he'd made, but why had he made a cross with Charlie's name on it?

Lizzie Sue knelt on the grass. Amos remained standing. "Here, Pa. Here's Charlie, come on down and see the cross. We put him here Pa. It's bin over a year now. There was a accident. Ye didn't mean ta do it. I know ye didn't. But it happened and now ye jist gotta remember. Ye gotta fergive yerself!" Lizzie Sue turned from the cross to look at her bewildered husband. His hands covered his face and his shoulders shook. "It's okay, Pa," said Lizzie Sue. "Charlie's with the angels."

Amos lowered his hands and Lizzie Sue realized she hadn't seen this crazed, unfocused look in Amos's eyes for a year. "No!" Amos shouted. "There weren't no accident! Quit tellin' me that! I gotta find Charlie. He's out there somewhere's and he's hurt." Amos ran toward the house. Ma looked after him, tears streaming down her face for the second time today.

She brought her apron up to her face and whispered into it, *Please don't do this, Pa. Don't leave me agin. I need ye here.*

She knelt silently by the cross and bowed her head to pray. *Charlie I know'd ye're gone to us forever but Pa cain't reckon with the idea of never seein' ye agin. I let him keep that boy I told ye about. He coulda bin yer twin and it seemed fer a while that we was a family agin. But it was wrong ta keep Ryan from his true family, and I helped him git away. Pa's gone after him. Help yer Pa, Charlie. Help them both.*

Chapter 31
2:16 p.m.

Jack rode into Mill Hollow on his chestnut mare. His mind kept going back to the boy Amos called Charlie. The mountain folk knew Amos hadn't been right in the head since he shot his boy. Lizzie Sue called it 'grievin' sickness,' but it was worse than that. *So who was that boy, and where'd he come from?* This question buzzed around Jack's head like skeeters in a swamp all the way down the mountain.

Despite these thoughts, when Jack finally got to town he was still surprised to see Charlie's likeness hung on a pole by the sheriff's office. Jack never learned to read, but looking at that boy's face on the poster told him something was wrong on the mountain. He tore the picture off the pole and strode into the Sheriff's office.

Ryan realized he was in better shape than he'd been before he got lost in the mountains. His legs felt powerful and his lungs had gotten used to the thinner mountain air. He thought about tearing up and down the soccer field and couldn't wait to get his life back. These thoughts kept him company on the faint trail made by Nearly and Amos when they had checked the traps. His heart jumped when he saw an eagle soaring overhead about fifty feet off to his right and there was the snowman rock! Ryan ran to the edge of the cliff and looked over. He was relieved to find out he hadn't been dreaming. The town was there, looking like a toy village waiting to be rearranged at a child's whim. It was the most beautiful sight he'd ever seen. He dropped the pail and

159

gun and lay on his belly soaking in the view below him. It was an incredibly steep drop, filled with sharp rocks and no real path.

He glanced over his shoulder at Lizzie Sue's pail and Charlie's gun. He'd never make it down with those. He sat up and pulled the pail toward him and ate the last of the cornbread. He drank what little water remained and knew it would be the water he'd miss most on his way down. He looked at his watch. In spite of being careful where he stepped, he had still made good time. It was only 2:33.

A strange thought came to him as he wiped his mouth with his sleeve. *I'm going to miss Lizzie Sue's cooking.* He pushed it aside, laughing. *I'll be having burgers and fries soon. I just started liking possum, rabbit and squirrel because there wasn't anything else to eat.* Ryan scanned the mountainside. Another eagle dipped and soared overhead. Wind whipped around and pine needles flew to the ground. Clouds scurried in the sky making it a perfect fall day. His hearing had become so in tune with the quiet that he could hear insects rubbing their legs, bees darting, birds crying and trees swaying. There would be many things he'd miss from the mountain: the stars at night, the crisp smell of the air, the absolute quiet, working in the garden, and Ma's berry cobbler. *Ma, why did I think of her that way?* He shook his head. He'd changed during his time on the mountain, both physically and emotionally. He had scars Ben wouldn't have. He'd also grown stronger, and thought his nose might look different from Ben's even though Ma had done her best to fix it for him. He was sure of himself, no longer the scared thirteen-year old boy, cowering behind a rock at the growling of a mountain lion. This independence and

160

confidence felt good. Then he wondered how Ben had changed? Maybe he had some new scars of his own. In Ryan's heart he knew his twin would still be like him where it mattered most, in their hearts.

A twig broke off to his left. Ryan grabbed the gun and clicked off the safety. A buck stepped into the clearing and looked lazily at him. He lowered the gun and the buck made his way out of the clearing. Feeling the heft of the gun and the racing of his heart reminded Ryan of the mountain lion he'd encountered, maybe even somewhere near this spot. He looked at the gun and knew it would just weigh him down. He also knew that Amos could be making his way here at this very minute. It was the thought of Amos that scared him more than encountering another mountain lion. He knew he needed to leave. He took the shells out, put them in his pocket and laid the gun carefully against a tree, next to the tin pail. *Maybe Amos will come by and find Charlie's gun and get some comfort from it.*

With that last thought Ryan searched out the best place to begin and lowered himself over the side. *I'm coming home Ben, can you feel it? I'm coming home!!*

Chapter 32

Ben pumped two more quarters into the video game. He fired at the targets jumping at him. Tony and Chris watched from behind. He heard his new companions cheering him on. His hands were on automatic, but his mind wandered off to Ryan. Although he'd been having a hard time connecting to his twin he still found himself thinking about Ryan constantly. *It didn't make sense.*

The line between himself and Ryan started getting fuzzy about a month ago, the same time he'd hooked up with the high-school dropouts. He was too busy being angry with his parents to understand why things were unraveling around him. He didn't yet realize the connection to his twin relied on their inner selves, on their similar attitudes and goals. He hadn't figured out the more he rebelled against who he was, the less he was able to connect to his twin. Instead he told himself, *I'd know if Ryan were dead. It's just a slump.*

"Come on! Come on!" Ben shouted, hitting the game with the palm of his hand, more out of internal frustration than over the game.

"Hey Ben, you're killing 'em. You're gonna get the high score today!" Tony put his hand on Ben's shoulder. "Loosen up man, you've got all day!"

Ben turned around and faced Tony and Chris. They *were* losers. They were sixteen and legally dropped out of school. He looked a lot like them with his black clothes, long hair, and ripped jeans. Besides their age, the biggest difference between Ben and the other boys was the number of piercings. Between all three of them there were eight, and

Ben only had one. A few months ago he and Ryan would have felt sorry for kids like them. Ryan used to say; "They're going nowhere fast." A part of Ben's mind wondered what he was doing with them – going nowhere too?

Then it hit him-*Ryan*-something was happening! Ryan was there, inside of him. He needed to be alone, far away from Tony and Chris and the constant beeping of the arcade. He ran out the door leaving the two losers standing with their mouths open.

"Kids," said Tony, "what do they know?" He stepped into the seat Ben vacated and gave all his limited attention to kickboxing the figures in front of him.

Chapter 33

Jack walked into the sheriff's office with the poster of Ryan in his hand. The deputy looked up and asked how he could help. "What do this paper say? Kin ye read it ta me?"

The deputy shifted his bulk out of the creaking chair and approached Jack. "It says; Missing, Ryan Burns. 13 years old. Lost June 25th in the mountains above Mill Hollow. Contact the sheriff. $10,000.00 reward if found." Jack's eyebrows shot up at the mention of a reward.

"That reward there, kin anybody git it if ye find the boy?"

"Yeah, if ye've got information about this boy that leads us ta him, you'll git the money."

"Well, I kin give ye that piece of information sir. Yessir, I kin." The deputy looked quizzically at the mountain man in front of the counter.

Ryan had only made his way down about sixty feet when he started sweating heavily. It was more difficult than he imagined when he'd been laying on his belly looking over the edge. He tried to remember to keep his mouth closed to avoid getting dirt in it and to keep it as moist as possible. He carefully searched each foothold before letting go to slide his hands lower. The fall nights were coming earlier and he knew, at this snail's pace, it was likely he wouldn't make it down before nightfall. He had learned first-hand that mountain dangers were real and he didn't want to risk a descent at night; it was tricky enough when he could look around for things to grab. He'd never be able to do it in the dark. His body urged him to get to Mill Hollow as fast as possible, but his mind slowed him down.

He began planning how to spend the night safely on the side of the mountain if it became necessary. He only let his mind think of it when he was resting against the mountain. Searching for a foothold took all of his concentration. He thought he'd be lucky to find a ledge or a cave, anything flat enough to sit on would do for one night. From what he could see there was nothing that remotely resembled a safe spot. Then he wondered if he'd been smart leaving the shotgun at the top of the mountain.

He became aware of his body again. His mouth was open and he gulped air. Just a few hours ago he'd thought he was in good shape. Now, as his muscles began to ache and his throat burned he felt something close to panic. He looked back up to see if he should go up instead of down and tried to calm himself. *Close your mouth, breathe normally. You can do this! Think what a good story this'll make when a teacher asks me to write about what I did over the summer. Keep going. Think happy thoughts. Ben, and Mom and Dad are waiting for me.* He kept up the mindless chatter until he felt calm enough to let go of his hold on the dirt and scrub weeds with his left hand and bring it level with his face. He dug another hold in before he brought his right hand down, and then his left foot. An eagle screeched overhead, sounding as lonely as Ryan felt.

Once outside the arcade door Ben turned left and ran until he came to an open park. He collapsed on one of the benches. A young mother and her baby moved farther away. His heart beat wildly and he drank air greedily, even though he'd run only a couple of blocks. He concentrated harder, *What is it, Ryan? I'm here, I feel you stronger than I have in a long time. What's happening?*

Ben closed his eyes, allowing the emotions to wash over him like gentle waves licking at his legs. He felt movement, fear, excitement, and something else. *What? What?* He couldn't get it. Ryan was doing something, but what? He raced for the bus stop. He needed to be home, in his bedroom - in their bedroom.

"Sheriff, I think ye'd better come out here. We may have a lead on the Burn's boy," announced the deputy. The Sheriff jumped to his feet and headed for the counter outside his office. He recognized Jack as one of the mountain people who came to town from time to time. He extended his hand and Jack shook it.

"You've got some information for us?"

"I kin tell ye where this boy is," snorted Jack, holding up the poster. "The deputy here says I git money if'n I tell ye."

"You'll get the money if we find Ryan. Where do you think you saw him?" The Sheriff had given up hope of ever finding the Burns' boy, believing he was dead. He kept putting up fresh posters only because the boy's twin sent them. With this news however, he was poised to fly into action.

"He's with Amos and Lizzie Sue Riley up the mountain a ways."

"You're telling me he's alive? How do you know it's this boy?" the Sheriff shot back.

166

"I seed him with these two eyes, jist a day ago." Jack pointed to his eyes. "I was over ta Amos and Lizzie's house on account a I was comin' ta town early this year 'cuz my Becca's havin' us a baby soon." Sheriff Martin wasn't sure he could stand still listening to this story unwind but he told himself to calm down and wait for the part that let him know this man really had seen Ryan Burns.

Jack droned on, "Miz Lizzie was all skittery-like and then Amos come home from checkin' his traps and he was with that boy in the picture there." Jack pointed again at the poster. "Amos called him Charlie."

"Charlie?" questioned the deputy.

"Yeah, Amos had a son named Charlie 'ceptin' I know Charlie's layin' in a grave by Amos' house."

"Did you talk to the boy?"

"No, Miz Lizzie sent him right off ta go herb pickin' or some such thin', but I got a good look at him, and this is him." Jack's finger pointed at the poster.

"Where's this place you saw Ryan?" asked the Sheriff.

"It's a good day's ride by horse, but I kin git ye there sooner if we took yer truck part way up and walked in the rest. We have ta hurry. I got me some tradin' ta do and supplies ta git, and a little wife who's scared ta be left alone fer long."

"That's not the only reason we have to hurry," said the deputy looking at his watch. "It'll be getting dark soon. I'll get us some gear and flashlights."

"I've got to make a phone call," said the Sheriff. Then he turned to Jack and said, "You, you've got about 15 minutes to get yer business done and then we're leaving."

167

Jack hurried out of the Sheriff's office thinking more about the reward than the supplies he needed to buy. He knew he'd never get his trading done in fifteen minutes but if everything worked out he'd have $10,000.00 soon – enough to buy whatever he and Becca needed for a long time.

3:26 p.m.

Ben lay on his bed with the lights off. There was a smile on his face and he was hugging his arms to himself. The connection he was feeling to Ryan was amazing. He could actually feel his twin coming closer. With every cell they had shared before birth he knew that his twin was coming home.

When he first got home and found no one there he'd run up to his bedroom and thrown his leather boots and vest on the floor and tried to connect with his brother. The connection came quickly. He sensed the outdoors; grasping at things, and…something else…fear? Yes, but hope too! It was an optimistic feeling, a feeling of expectation surrounding Ryan. He hadn't felt anything like this for so long and he was positive now that his twin was coming home.

He jumped from his bed, startled as he heard the angry voice of his mother. "Ben! Ben! Are you here? Get down here this minute!" Ben pulled open his door, not bothering to lock it, and bounded down the stairs. "You weren't at school today. Where were you?"

"It doesn't matter, Mom. Ryan's on his way home!" He hugged her and repeated, "He's coming home!"

"What are you talking about?" Her voice conveyed annoyance.

168

"I feel it mom. We're connected again."

"Come on Ben! Don't play me! I've had it with you today."

"I know I've been acting strange, I'm sorry but you've got to believe me - Ryan's coming home!" Just then the phone rang and startled both of them. Mrs. Burns turned to answer it. Ben stopped her, "Let the machine get it, mom. We need to talk."

Ben walked toward the family room expecting his mom to follow. After the fourth ring he heard the familiar voices of his family saying, "Hi, you've reached the Burn's home. We can't get to the phone right now. Leave a message and we'll get back to you." No one had changed the phone message and every time Ben heard it pain raced through his heart – but not this time. After the beep came the unmistakable southern drawl of Sheriff Martin.

"Mr. and Mrs. Burns, and Ben, this is Sheriff Martin." Sarah was at the phone and pressed the stop button on the answering machine as she shouted into the phone.

"I'm here! Don't hang up. It's Ryan, isn't it?" Ben was at her side and barely able to breathe.

"I don't want to get your hopes up, but we've got a man here who says he saw a boy in the mountains that looks like Ryan. Says he saw him a day ago."

Sarah felt weak in the knees and the room began to swirl. She sat down on the floor. Clutching the phone in one hand, she reached out to Ben with the other and grabbed his knee. "He's alive?"

"We're not sure the boy in question is Ryan, but we're on our way to check it out. There's no need for you to come to Mill Hollow. We'll call you later."

"No!" shouted Sarah. "Of course we'll be there. We'll be there! Go find him!"

Chapter 34

Amos wandered around the mountain for an hour before he thought of the nesting place. *Maybe Charlie's there, lookin' at the village, jist like he done when he was little.* He turned Nearly to the left and headed toward the aerie.

Ryan's hands were raw from digging into the hard dirt, rocks and weeds. His nails were so packed with mountain earth that his fingernails pulled away from the skin, making every hand movement hurt. He was light-headed and his muscles and lungs were raw. He needed to rest again but he was making such slow progress. He brought his hand next to his face and glanced at his watch. There wouldn't be much light left and he hadn't found a place he might sit for the night. He tried not to panic. He hadn't gotten this far to lose it now.

Amos stepped off Nearly and walked toward the cliff. He spied something on the ground and in the next few steps recognized Ma's berry pail and one of her glass jars. There were paper wrappings inside. Amos sniffed them and knew it was Ma's stew. He looked past the pail and saw Charlie's gun leaning against the tree. *Charlie's bin here!*

"Charlie!" he shouted down the mountain. "Charlie? Kin ye hear me?" The sounds rumbled over and over down the mountainside and fell on Ryan's ears.

Amos, he breathed. *No, not now. God, please don't let him see me. I should have hidden the gun and pail! That was stupid! He can't get me now – not when I've come this far!*

Amos' gruff voice echoed around him again, cascading through the ravine. "Chaaaarlieeee!"

"Ted, Ben and I are leaving for Mill Hollow, with or without you!" Sarah clutched the phone to her ear. Veins stood out on her neck and she tapped her foot. Every ounce of her body was wired to go."

"It's only a lead, Sarah. Even if we make the best possible time it will take us at least ten hours to get there. That means we'll be there somewhere around three tomorrow morning."

"I can do the math Ted!"

"All I'm saying is that we should wait until morning to see if this lead even goes anywhere. You may just be setting yourself up for a fall. If it's a good lead we can leave tomorrow right after school. We'll have the whole weekend ahead of us."

Sarah paced back and forth. "I'm not arguing anymore, Ted! Ben and I are out of here in thirty minutes. We'd like you to come with us, but we *are* going." Sarah hit the end call button and slammed it on the counter. She ran upstairs to put on jeans and grab an overnight bag. *I'll call for a substitute in the car,* she thought to herself as her shaking hands tried to unbutton her dress. *I should change the message machine to let Ryan or the sheriff know when we left.* Hope soared through her. She hadn't felt this good since their ill-fated vacation when the four of them had been laughing around the campfire.

"This is as far as we kin go by truck," said Jack. The statement came as no surprise to the Sheriff who wondered how much farther his four-wheel drive would have made it anyway. "We go on foot from now on. Ye kin park yer truck over there." Jack motioned to the side of some trees. "Don't nobody hardly know 'bout this trail," he mumbled.

Jack, Sheriff Martin, and the Deputy gathered flashlights and the rescue backpacks from the back of the Ford. They set out with Jack in front, leading them up what he called a trail, but if there was a path, the Sheriff couldn't see it. The fat deputy just shook his head and hoped he could keep up with the other two.

Their going wasn't as rough as Ryan's since they could easily go upright, single file, using rocks, stumps and roots for help. If Ryan had known about this trail, only about 400 feet to his right, he would have made much better time.

Ryan heard the call for Charlie over and over and over. Each echo shooting down the mountain was like a slap to his consciousness. It took all his concentration to keep moving carefully when what he really wanted to do was run. *Okay, just keep going. Keep three of your appendages connected at all times.* Ryan was thankful that his dad had made them practice on rock walls before their vacation. He glanced both ways, still looking for a safe resting place. *Go away Amos. Please just go away. Go back to Lizzie Sue and leave me alone!* Ryan prayed this, like a mantra, over and over in his head as he lowered his body inches at a time.

His left foot struck something more solid. He moved his foot out farther behind him and the hardness continued. He shuffled his foot left and right and decided it was a ledge

173

at least wide enough for him to step on and take a breath without needing to hang on to the mountain. He carefully let the weight of one foot come to rest on the rock, and then gently lowered the other foot. He let go of his right hand next and finally his left came to rest at his side. His body began to relax as he felt his muscles loosen. He stood, facing the mountain until his ragged breathing slowed down. It felt wonderful to stand on something solid and he relished the moment. Having his arms down at his side felt like the moment just before he fell asleep when his head burrowed deeper into the pillow. He jerked his body, he couldn't afford to relax that much.

On his descent, looking sideways was scary enough, so Ryan hadn't tried looking down. Now he glanced behind him and saw the ledge he was standing on was actually quite a large outcropping of rock, fairly flat and smooth. He looked left and then right and estimated it was about six feet long and maybe twice as wide. *This would be a perfect place to rest for the night if Amos wasn't trailing me.* He wiped the sweat from his face and brushed his bruised and cut hands on his pant legs. He rested against the side of the mountain and allowed his eyes to close for a few seconds to keep focused and think about what to do next.

"Charlie! I'm comin' fer ye. Stay still! I kin git ye back home. I won't let nothin' bad happen to ye!" Ryan felt a clump of dirt hit him first, and then a shower of dirt and rocks rained down on him.

Amos is coming down after me! Ryan looked around desperately and noticed for the first time that around the corner of rock the ground seemed to level off. There was a slight trail leading to the left not too far from the ledge he was on. All he needed to do was work his way horizontally about two feet from the ledge and then lower himself as he'd been doing just a few more feet to get to the place where there was better footing. From what he could see of the trail he might be able to walk it face first, which would be much faster, even if he had to walk crab-like for a while. *It's got to lead somewhere, most likely to Mill Hollow,* thought Ryan. More rocks fell from above and bounced around him. They were coming faster now and several larger ones barely missed him as they hit the ledge he was standing on.

It was starting to get dark and he wondered if he should stay here, relatively safe, hoping Amos would give up, or somehow miss him on his way down; or if he should try to work his way to the trail and maybe beat Amos to town? He was quiet sitting on this rock and getting to the trail would be noisy. It would be harder to miss him if he was making noise. *Think this through!* What he heard next made his skin crawl.

"Kin ye hear me Charlie? I didn't mean ta shoot ye. Ye jist sneaked up on me. I'll never hairt ye agin, I promise. I'm comin' ta git ye and bring ye home ta yer ma!"

Amos killed Charlie! He's even crazier than I thought. I can't let him see me!

5:39 p.m.

Ted made it home just as Ben and Sarah were pulling out of the garage. He squealed his car to a stop next to Sarah's and jumped out. He loosened his tie and opened the driver's side of his wife's car. "Move over, Sarah. I've made this trip a lot more often than you. I can do it in my sleep."

175

Sarah unbuckled her seatbelt and moved over to the passenger side. Ben had gotten into the backseat as soon as he saw his dad. Ted took off his jacket and tie and tossed them both in the backseat. "Take care of these, will you Ben?" Ben felt tears sting his eyes at this simple request. Maybe his dad didn't believe anything would come of this trip, but at least he was with them, and that was enough for now.

The first couple hours in the car were tense. No one said much of anything until finally Ted asked who was hungry? Sarah shook her head and Ben said, "No thanks."

"Well, we've got to keep our energy up. I'll drive off the next exit we come to. Sarah sighed loudly and looked at her watch, momentarily wishing that Ted hadn't made it home before they left. Seeing his wife's perturbed gesture made Ted shake his head and lean closer toward the car door, away from his wife.

Ben saw this exchange between his parents and said, "I changed my mind Dad. I'm hungry. I could go for a couple of burgers. It'll only take a few minutes at the drive-through window. That won't matter will it Mom?" Ben's voice was pleading. Sarah gathered all of the good feelings she could muster, and put her hand on Ted's arm.

"Sure honey, I could eat something too."

Chapter 35

Lizzie Sue had long ago taken Pa's dinner plate off the table. When the sun disappeared an evening chill set in and she walked the few steps to stoke the fire. She wasn't so much worried for Amos as she was for Ryan. *Is he gittin' fer enough down afore Pa gits ta him? Is he lost or layin' somewhere's hairt?* She couldn't make herself stop thinking about Ryan and her husband. She knew Amos would either be okay or he would go deeper into his grievin' sickness. There was nothing much she could do for him now other than pray. She searched her mind, *Did I do all I could fer the boy?*

Twigs snapped outside and Lizzie Sue knew someone was coming toward the house. She raced out the door shouting, "Pa! Pa!"

"Miz Lizzie, it's me, Jack"

Jack, thought Lizzie Sue, *What's he doin' here?* Jack was the first to come out of the trees just beyond the house. Then Lizzie Sue saw two strangers, both dressed alike and carrying guns, pointed at her. Jack was carrying a lantern of some kind she'd never seen before and was shining it in her face. One of the two men she didn't know was sweating badly and looked sickly.

Time stood still, and then lengthened creating unbearable feelings of fear, anger, and confusion. Lizzie Sue's hands flew to her mouth.

"Charlie, talk ta me! Where ye be? Ye ain't hairt are ye?" Ryan sat on his haunches, listening to Amos creep closer to him. He was working himself toward the end of the ledge. Rocks continued to fall around him, pinging where he huddled. Amos' voice seemed like it was right on top of him. Then he heard a change in Amos' noisy climbing. More rocks, larger ones, began to hit the ledge, some just barely missing Ryan. In the next instant, before he had time to stand up, Ryan heard a sliding sound and a terrible piercing scream.

Sarah tried her best to eat the burger and fries from their stop. The little bit she choked down was rumbling and gurgling in her stomach and she wasn't sure if she'd keep it down.

"Are you okay Mom?"

Ben's voice penetrated the fuzz in her head, "What, Honey?"

"Are you okay? You don't look like you feel good."

"I'm okay, just excited and nervous. How about you?" Sarah turned to look at her son.

"I'm fine Mom, never been better." Sarah smiled at him and realized he had put on 'normal' Ben clothes. The 'old' Ben that is. He had on an NYU sweatshirt and jeans that were reasonably clean. He'd even taken out his earring and put his hair back into a ponytail.

"You look nice Honey," Sarah smiled at her son. "Did I ever tell you that your dad had a ponytail when I first met him?"

"No way!" screeched Ben.

Ted tried to enter into this banter, "What? You don't think I was young and hip?"

Can our lives be this normal again? Sarah wondered. *Dear God, please let Ryan be with the Sheriff when we get to Mill Hollow. We need him to make us whole.* She tried to refocus on the conversation.

"How long did your hair get Dad?"

"I don't know, what do you think Sarah?"

"Maybe down to here," Sarah answered, touching a spot in the middle of Ted's back as he leaned forward.

"No way!" Laughed Ben. "Do you think Ryan's hair will be as long as mine? Do you think he'll have his hair in a ponytail too?"

Both parents said nothing, lost in their reactions to Ben's question. Sarah thought, *Ben's put his life on hold until Ryan comes back. How could I have missed what he was doing? The signs were all there, skipping school, not wanting new clothes or a haircut. Not even wanting to go out for soccer. The more we pushed the more he rebelled. He's been searching for a new identity, one that he could shed when Ryan came back. He didn't want to experience life as it could be until Ryan was with him.* Sarah didn't think this had been a conscious effort on Ben's part but she now saw *him* for the first time since they came back from the mountain. *By worrying about Ryan, I've ignored Ben's pleas for help.* Sarah realized that her son probably felt like he'd only been half-alive. *How could I have let him down by telling him I didn't believe Ryan would return?* She let a few tears trickle down her cheeks, promising herself she'd make it up to him, whether or not this trip led to Ryan.

Ted was thinking too. He wondered how he could keep his family together when Mill Hollow turned out to be another dead-end. *There's no way Ryan's alive. How could he be? Where would he have been all this time?*

Sarah took off her seatbelt and turned around toward her son. She reached out and touched him. "Honey, Ryan will still look like you. You'll see when we get to Mill Hollow." Ben had scooted forward in his seat and now slid back with a smile on his face. "I know mom." He loved hearing the words anyway.

Ted took in the exchange between his wife and son, and his voice came out gruffer than he meant when he said, "Sarah, you'd better put your seatbelt on. I'm going pretty fast and I don't need to worry about you." Sarah turned around to put her seatbelt on, and gave Ted's arm a squeeze.

Chapter 36

"Ye got nothin' ta fear Miz Lizzie. We're jist lookin' fer Amos," said Jack.

"Ma'am, I'm Sheriff Martin, and this is my deputy. Is your husband home?"

Lizzie Sue wasn't sure she could talk at first. She'd never been good around strangers, and these strangers were pointing guns at her. The Sheriff holstered his weapon and the Deputy took his lead and did the same. Jack spoke again, "Miz Lizzie, where's that curly haided boy who was with Amos yesterday?"

Lizzie Sue's heart was pounding as thoughts flew through her head. *What do these people want? What's he mean I ain't got nothin' to be afeared of?* The strangers were now only about ten feet from her. She looked longingly back at the safety of her home. Someone was talking to her again but she missed it. She couldn't think straight, and didn't know what to say.

"Ma'am, are you okay?" It was the Sheriff. He had taken her arm and was leading all of them into the house. "Can you help us find Ryan Burns? He's the boy on this poster." The Sheriff unfolded the worn paper and gave it to Lizzie Sue. "His parents and brother miss him dearly. You can understand that, can't you Ma'am?" Lizzie Sue thought she'd faint dead away at the sight of Charlie - no, Ryan - staring at her from the paper. Something broke inside of her and she started talking.

"He's gone ta Mill Hollow," Lizzie Sue responded softly.

"Is he with Amos?" asked Jack.

"No, Ryan started off alone, but Amos is out lookin' fer him."

"Do you know which way they went, Ma'am?"

Lizzie Sue looked up at the Sheriff. He had kind eyes and she could see he wanted to help. "Ryan went ta the eagle's nestin' place. I guess Amos prob'ly figgered that out by now."

"Eagles?" questioned the Sheriff looking at Jack.

There's an eagle nestin' place a few miles from here. I kin take ye. It's up the mountain from where we parked the truck," answered Jack. "It won't be hard with them flashlights. I know this mountain like I know the back a my hand."

Sheriff Martin looked back to Lizzie Sue again. "Ma'am, do you need to do anything in the house? We'll have to ask you to come with us."

Lizzie Sue's eyes widened and Jack stumbled over his words going to her defense, "No, I mean, ah....Now look here Sheriff, I kin take ye there without botherin' Miz Lizzie here. She don't need ta come with us."

The Sheriff looked at Jack with cold eyes, "Do you think I like dragging her out of her house this time of night anymore than you do? But she's a part of this and I'm not leaving her up here just to have to come back and get her later." He motioned to Lizzie Sue. "Go on Ma'am, do what you have to. Close up your house."

Lizzie Sue looked around the small cabin, walked over to the stove and took off the coffee kettle. Using a worn towel she placed the kettle carefully on an oak slab Pa had carved. Her hand brushed the likeness of a rabbit he'd chiseled into it, just to make it fancy for her. She took a black, knitted shawl off a peg on the wall, and snuffed out the kitchen lantern before starting out the door.

Chapter 37

Everything was still after the piercing scream before more falling rocks hit Ryan. They made him jump and he almost lost his grip. He grabbed the side of the mountain to steady himself. He searched the darkness above him and saw Amos clinging to a handful of gnarled roots. Both his feet were dangling in the air. Ryan knew the roots wouldn't hold the big man long, but he could only think about getting away. He edged himself over to his left to leave the ledge and get back onto the mountain. He was torn between hurrying and going slow enough to make sure he didn't fall. He looked up again and he could see Amos' hands slipping.

"Charlie, are ye hairt?" screamed Amos. Ryan ignored him and kept inching sideways toward where he hoped he could reach the trail a few yards below. His heart raced and he broke out in a sweat. He was as close to panic as he'd ever been.

"Charlie? Charlie?" Ryan tried not to hear the pleading in Amos' voice. "Charlie, move out the way I cain't hold much longer and...." Another scream pierced the night and then a dull thud shook the ledge about a foot away from Ryan. He didn't bother to look back; he just started moving faster. There was one thing on his mind – escape!

He made it a foot or so off the ledge and then began feeling around with his toes to find a foothold to start back down. *I'm so close, I can't let him get me now. I've got to get to the trail.* These thoughts filled Ryan's mind and not the fact that everything around him was completely still. Amos wasn't talking, much less moving to grab him. Ryan stopped moving too, poised between escape and curiosity. He listened before tentatively saying, "Amos, are you okay?" There was no response. "Amos can you hear me?" There was still no response. Every muscle in Ryan's body was poised to go down the mountain and get to the trail, but something wouldn't let him move. He refused to look behind him at what was on the ledge, he didn't want to see Amos. He tried something else, calling out again, "Pa? Pa? Can you hear me?" Even calling out this name that he swore he would never use again, got no response. He listened so hard his ears hurt, and then he heard a faint moan, more like a whimper. *Is that Amos? Is he hurt?* Ryan's body needed to keep moving. He didn't want to think about Amos, but his mind wouldn't let him leave it alone. *I can't leave him without knowing what happened.* He rested his head against the mountain for a few seconds and then took a deep breath and turned back to look at Amos.

What he saw was worse than he imagined. "I'm coming Pa. Can you hear me?" Ryan hoped using the name Pa instead of Amos might help calm the man. Ryan moved himself more firmly onto the ledge and looked at Amos lying still. Then Ryan looked up to the scrub pine where Amos had just been and guessed it was a thirty-foot drop onto the ledge. There was a good chance Amos was dead.

"Oh God, oh God, oh God," Ryan wasn't sure whether he was praying or yelling but he repeated it over and over as he knelt down to touch Amos. When his hand rested on the rock he felt something warm and wet. For a moment it didn't register what it was. Then it hit him; it was blood and a lot of it. He jerked his hand up and wiped it on his pants. "Oh God, oh God, oh God!" he started again. He couldn't

185

leave Amos like this. "What do I do?" Then Lizzie Sue slipped into his mind and he saw her ministering and knew what he had to do: find out where the blood was coming from by moving his hands around on Amos. Touching him wasn't something Ryan relished so he took a deep breath. In the dark of the evening he moved his hands slowly over Amos' crumpled body feeling for a wound.

He would have given anything not to be doing this. He didn't like being so close to this man. Ryan's nerves were stretched as tight as a rubber band as he envisioned Amos' strong hand reaching out to encircle his wrist. He was making his way down the left leg when he found the source of blood. He recoiled in horror and wiped his hand on his own pants. He'd touched a bone sticking out of Amos's leg. Ryan gagged and looked around, wondering what to do next. A moan escaped Amos' lips. Ryan had to think fast or the man who had both saved his life, and made it miserable, would die.

From watching television, and the health classes at school he knew wounds needed pressure to stop bleeding, but he wasn't sure if this was the same when a bone was sticking out. He had to try something so he quickly unbuttoned his shirt and tore off one of the arms. It didn't come off as easily as he thought it would and he ended up biting at it with his teeth. He wrapped it around Amos's leg just above where the bone jutted out, and tied it, but not too tightly. He did the same thing with the other sleeve, and then tore the rest of the shirt into large lengths and tied those around the leg also. He didn't know if this would help slow down the blood flow, but it was all he could think to do.

He shivered at the cool fall night and realized he'd be cold going down the mountain without a shirt. Too late, he thought about the scrapes and cuts he'd get on his chest without the cloth protection. He wished he'd used Amos's shirt, but knew people needed to be kept warm when they were hurt. He bent close to Amos's ear and whispered. "Pa, I'm going to get some help. Don't give up, Lizzie Sue needs you." With that Ryan wiped his hands on his pants and started off the ledge once again, wondering if he would make it to town in time for Amos to live.

9:58 p.m.

The tension in the Burns' car tightened as it approached the halfway point to Mill Hollow; each person lost in his or her own thoughts. Sarah looked at her watch. It would be about five more hours before they got there. Those five hours were going to be the longest she'd ever spent.

Ben was thinking about school and how he'd been acting lately. He came to the conclusion that his behavior had been a form of stalling, of not wanting to experience things without Ryan. It sounded kind of dumb to him as it rolled around his head, but he knew that's what he'd been doing. He wouldn't need to pretend anymore. He and Ryan would be together again soon. He could start eighth grade all over again, and this time he'd do it right.

Ted was worried about the disappointment his wife and son would feel once they reached Mill Hollow and found nothing. He hoped this trip put an end to their doubts about Ryan. It's the only reason he'd raced home to go with them. He promised himself this would be the last trip he'd make to Mill Hollow.

The Sheriff was surprised at the good time they were making walking toward the eagle's nesting place. He looked at Lizzie Sue admiringly. *She may be a little thing, but she sure is tough! I wonder if she has any idea what lies ahead for her and her husband if they've truly kept Ryan Burns against his will all these months. Kidnapping's a serious crime.*

Through the dark, Lizzie Sue spotted Nearly nibbling grass and she looked around for Amos. Then she saw the berry pail tipped on its side. She let Jack attend to the horse while she made her way to the pail. Earlier she thought of trying to talk Jack into leading them somewhere else, maybe give Amos more time to do whatever it was he set out to do. Even before that thought was fully formed she knew she wouldn't interfere with Jack's directions. She called him over to her and showed him the spot where Ryan, and probably Amos, had started down the mountain.

The Sheriff sized up the situation and went over to the gun leaning against the tree. He sniffed the barrel. It hadn't been fired recently. Next he walked over to Jack and Lizzie Sue and picked up the food wrappers in the pail and inspected them. "Is this food from your home, Ma'am?"

"I give it ta Ryan afore he left this mornin'," answered Lizzie Sue, feeling good that Ryan had eaten it all.

"You *gave* it to him?" The Sheriff had a puzzled look on his face.

"He needed food, didn't he? If'n he was goin' ta git away."

"Get away?" questioned the Sheriff.

"Miz Lizzie," broke in Jack, "Ye got some talkin' ta do."

"I ain't sayin' another word 'til my man's safe." In her head she added, *And my Ryan, too!*

Nearly snuffled over to Lizzie Sue. Her ears were bent back, wondering who these people were. Lizzie Sue took hold of her bridle and stroked her nose.

"That's Amos' horse," Jack said. "Amos wouldn't leave her fer no good reason. If'n they both went down the mountain this way they mighta come to the trail we come up on." Jack reached for one of the flashlights and held it over the edge. "This way is a might dangerous Miz Lizzie. Don't Amos know that?"

"I reckon he knows it all right, but Ryan don't know any other way. And I ain't never bin down there neither."

"Amos!" Jack shouted, cupping his hands around his mouth. His voice echoed down and reached Amos's ears. Amos stirred to answer back, but nothing came out. Jack tried one more time, but there was still no answer.

The deputy was the first to speak. "They're out of reach, or worse."

Sheriff Martin looked at his watch, pressing the button to illuminate the dial. 10:38. "Jack can you get us back to our car from here?"

"I kin do that, just soon's we drop Miz Lizzie off back home."

"She'll be coming with us," answered the Sheriff, looking at Lizzie Sue to see her reaction.

Jack snuck a look at Lizzie Sue too. Her face was white, her features frozen in a mask of bewilderment. "That'll save us a might bit a time. It shore will," answered

Jack, wondering if he'd done the right thing by going to the Sheriff. Mountain folk didn't usually mess with town folk. Maybe Becca'd been right. The thought of Becca turned Jack's stomach. She'd soon be getting worried about him. *All's I kin do now is stick close ta Miz Lizzie and see her through this.* He adjusted the beam on the flashlight and led them to a much safer and quicker route down the mountain and back to the truck.

Jack held Lizzie Sue's arm to escort her down the mountain trail a few hundred feet to the right of where Amos and the boy had gone down. It was going to be rough, Lizzie's first time off the mountain. Jack gave Nearly a spank and told her to get home. She galloped off, glad to be away from the strangers.

Ryan made it to the trail, but not without many new cuts and scrapes on his bare chest. He stopped once to lean on his knees and catch his breath. He waited until his sides stopped heaving and his throat felt less constricted. While he was running he'd gone right past the Sheriff's truck hidden in the brush and trees. He never noticed it. He was intent on one thing only, getting to Mill Hollow. Not only his life depended on it, but now Amos's life too. He had to keep going!

"We're making great time," said Ted to Sarah. She glanced at the digital clock above their silent CD player. It blinked 12:29 p.m. "We should be in Mill Hollow in about three more hours at this rate."

Sarah smiled at Ted. But he couldn't see it in the darkness of the car. Thankfully, Ben had fallen asleep and lay sprawled on the back seat like a rumpled piece of discarded bedding.

Jack hadn't let go of Lizzie Sue's arm since they'd left Eagle Rock. It took them a little over two hours of brisk walking to get back to the truck. Jack admired Miz Lizzie's spunk as he helped her into the backseat of the vehicle. This would be her first ride in a car, but she wouldn't be enjoying it.

Jack's thoughts went to his own wife. He was conflicted. He knew Becca would be worried, but he also knew he couldn't leave Lizzie Sue alone. *I've got ta make sure she's okay afore I kin git back home.* He hadn't even thought about the fact that his horse was still in front of the Sheriff's office, and he hadn't gotten most of his provisions yet.

Chapter 38

Now that Ryan was at the bottom of the mountain he looked back up and wondered how he'd done it. He was breathing hard and his body trembled. At least one of the cuts on his chest dripped blood. He wiped at it half-heartedly then gave up. What bothered him most were his hands. They were torn to shreds, bleeding under the nails and throbbing intensely. He wanted to cry, not just a few tears, but a really good cry, except there was no time for it. He looked at his watch - just past midnight.

The full moon helped him get down the mountain and now it illuminated the way into town. He wished it could also give him help for his sore muscles. They twitched and ached in places he had no idea *could* ache. He looked at the dirt road stretching out before him and thought of the yellow brick road from The Wizard of Oz . *I could use a tin man, lion and scarecrow about now.* He laughed out loud at the thought of him in ruby slippers saying, "There's no place like home. There's no place like home." The sound of his laugh in the quiet night helped settle his nerves and he started off again, this time at a slow trot. It was all he could muster.

His stomach begged for food, his tongue felt too big for his mouth and his lungs were raw. An owl hooted somewhere in the distance, and this time it didn't sound ominous, it sounded encouraging. *Yoooou can do it. Yoooou can do it. Yoooou can do it.* Ryan remembered one of his favorite books from childhood and with each step he told himself, *I know I can! I know I can! I know I can!*

Lizzie Sue still hadn't spoken a word. Inside the truck she gripped Jack's hand as hard as she could but every bump and jerk in the road made her gasp. Jack couldn't think of anything to say to her, so he just let her hang on. He knew they'd be in town soon enough. He sighed and looked around at the scenery changing from rugged mountain to gentle forest.

The first building Ryan came to was a gas station. Even though he remembered how old fashioned this small southern town had seemed to him on their way to the mountain, it now seemed modern and fresh after months in Lizzie Sue and Amos' cabin. The gas station was closed up tight. He stopped and allowed himself to breathe in the station's smells – gasoline, cars, cool cement, and stale exhaust. The store's subdued lights illuminated the inside counters and showed an array of candy, chips, and gum. He took a few precious seconds to look through the window. Then something jumped out at him. A poster of himself was taped to the cash register. He couldn't read the small print but he could make out the large word 'REWARD'. The poster nearly broke his resolve. *People are looking for me!* Of course Ryan had known his family would be looking for him, but this validated all his hard work. He was free now. He wanted to pull open the door, rip down the poster and take it shouting through the streets. *Look! It's me! I'm alive! Help me!* Instead he laid his head against the cool glass of the door until the hum of the soft drink machine broke through the fog inside his brain and buzzed in his ears.

"Coke machine!" His mouth watered and it was all he could do to make himself move on.

He crossed the street to a hardware store. Not even a light was on but next to the door was an old fashioned outdoor telephone. Ryan raced over and punched in 911. He waited. Nothing happened. His heart raced as he hung up and punched the numbers again. Still nothing. *Town's probably not even hooked up to 911.* He hung up the phone and looked around. A grocery store next door also had a poster of him in the window and he touched it as he went by. A diner and a Laundromat completed one side of town. He caught a glimpse of himself in the Laundromat windows and was shocked at his reflection. He looked wild without a shirt and long hair sticking out every which way. His face was streaked with grime and he didn't like what he saw. *People might not even recognize me from that poster anymore.* As he crossed the street to the other side he expected tumbleweeds to roll over him, so dead was the feeling in the streets. He scanned the short block and tried to focus his attention on what he was doing. *What am I doing?* he wondered. He was losing it. He told himself to hold on, he couldn't give in to exhaustion and fear this close to the end of his journey. He shouted out loud, "Is anybody home? I need some help!" He waited for an answer and when none came he staggered to the first building on the other side of the street. There was a sign out front that said, 'Dr. Will Tebo, M.D.' He turned in a circle again scanning for any sign of life. A telephone pole in front of the Doctor's office had another poster of him tacked to it. Ryan ripped the poster off the pole and held it tightly in his hand as a kind of good luck charm.

Next to that building was the Sheriff's office, but there were no lights there either. The last store in town was a darkened drugstore where he spotted another poster advertising his disappearance. He was everywhere he looked. Next to the drugstore was a small picnic area with swings. *Swings?* They looked so peaceful to Ryan that he wanted to curl up next to the playground and sleep; just wait for one of the nice people who put his picture in their window to find him in the morning. He started toward the swings, and then remembered Amos. No one would find Amos if he didn't tell someone where he was. "I can do it. I can do it. I can do it."

Ryan walked to the Sheriff's office and pounded on the door. He waited and pounded again. Nothing. It was a ghost town. He felt like he was in the Twilight Zone where time stood still, and everyone except him was sleeping off an alien curse.

He was hungry, tired, and very close to becoming delirious. He wondered if he'd done the right thing by leaving Amos on the rock ledge. He sat on the two steps in front of the Sheriff's office, hung his arms over his knees and looked around. The four streetlights ended at the last building. Ryan looked at his watch, 1:27 a.m. *What time would a town like this wake up?* He guessed it would be around 6:00. He could wait that long, but Amos couldn't. He struggled to his feet, deciding to start in on the houses across the street from the small park.

He approached an ancient looking red brick house. Ryan's heart pounded as he walked up the four cement steps onto the covered porch. He shivered now that he had slowed down from his run into town. There was a cozy looking swing on the porch and somehow that gave Ryan hope. He

195

looked for a doorbell but didn't find one so he knocked on the screen doorframe. It was a weak knock and he knew it so he opened the screen door and knocked harder on the oak door, with his palm flat against the wood. He pounded for a long time and began shouting again. "Is anybody home?"

The answer he got came in the form of a barking dog. He followed the barking with his ears, and stepped off the porch. Ryan was met by a man of about sixty, with a shotgun in one hand and the leash of the barking dog in the other. The man's robe flapped under a coat, which was buttoned wrong, leaving part of the coat longer on one side. His hair stuck out only from the sides of his head because the rest was bald. He was chewing on a toothpick.

Ryan stopped at the bottom of the porch stairs, sized up the man and wished the person with the porch swing had answered the door.

"What you doin' there, boy? Those folks ain't home."

"I need help."

"What kind of help you need this time a night, boy? Where's your shirt?"

How could Ryan explain everything to this man while he was holding a gun on him? Ryan looked down and realized once again that he hardly recognized himself and then he remembered the posters all over town and the one he'd stuck in his pocket. He took it out and showed it to the man. "This is me! I've been lost for a long time, well, not exactly lost." He wasn't making any sense. "There's a man on the mountain who fell and he's hurt bad! He needs a doctor and we need to get him to a hospital. Do you have a car?"

"You expect me to go into the mountains this time a night? You must be as crazy as you look!" The man spat on the sidewalk without losing his toothpick.

"You don't understand!" wailed Ryan. He hadn't gotten this far, and endured months of captivity just to be thwarted by a grouchy old man.

"Oh, I understand," interrupted the man lowering his gun and telling his dog to stop. The barking animal quieted and even started wagging his tail. "I just ain't gonna do it. I *will* let you use my phone to call the Sheriff." He turned and expected Ryan to follow. Ryan thought for a few seconds, at least he thought as hard as his muddled mind would let him think. In the end he decided he really had no choice but to follow this man into his house to use the phone.

I hope he's nicer than he looks, prayed Ryan, uneasy to put himself in the hands of another stranger.

They hadn't walked more than twenty or thirty feet when car lights pierced the blackness of the street. The dog remained quiet but turned in the opposite direction, straining at his leash to sniff the approaching vehicle. Ryan turned around to see if it was someone who might look friendlier than this man. He shielded his eyes from the brightness of the lights. The truck stopped in front of the Sheriff's Office.

"That'll be the Sheriff right there," pointed out the man with the gun. "You best git over to see him." Ryan thanked the man and limped down the sidewalk. He'd made it halfway to the truck when the Sheriff and the deputy got out.

"Sheriff! Sheriff!" yelled Ryan. The two officers spun around as Jack got Lizzie Sue out of the back seat. Ryan stopped about ten feet from the truck when he saw her step off the running board. He felt disoriented at the sight of her with the man he'd seen in the window at the cabin. It was like all the hours he'd spent trying to get away from the mountain hadn't happened. He expected to see Amos come out of the truck next.

The Sheriff walked over to the filthy boy and looked at him. "You're Ryan Burns aren't you, son?" All Ryan could do was shake his head yes because his eyes were still fixed on Lizzie Sue who looked almost as worn and disoriented as he did.

"What have you done to Lizzie Sue?" shouted Ryan, although his voice came out more like a raspy whisper. He walked over to stand next to the frail woman who looked out of place off her mountain. The effort hurt but he raised his arm and draped it around her protectively.

Jack scratched his head in wonderment at the boy who looked like Charlie.

Lizzie Sue turned to Ryan and whimpered, "Are ye hairt bad? Is Pa okay?" She was already touching the gashes on Ryan's chest.

Jack jumped in with his own questions, "Where's Amos boy? Did he come after ye?"

"He's about halfway down the mountain, coming from the eagle's nests…just before…just before the trail into town. He's on a rock ledge. He fell coming after me, and he's hurt." He looked at Jack as he spoke, but now he turned to Lizzie Sue and held her away from him. "He's hurt Lizzie Sue. I don't know how badly, but he's hurt. He's not moving and his leg's bleeding. I fixed it the best I could with my shirt and then I came for help."

Lizzie Sue clutched at Ryan. "Take me ta him, Ryan. I jist got ta help him. Help me git ta him!" Lizzie Sue seemed to have gained back some of her strength.

"The only ledge I know that big is near the same trail we jist come down on Sheriff. He must be a ways above where we parked the car," said Jack. "I kin go back with the deputy ta git Amos."

The Sheriff turned to his deputy and said, "Get Doc Tebo to go with you. I'll call for an ambulance to meet you back here."

The two men took off and the Sheriff turned his attention to Ryan and Lizzie Sue. "Are you okay son?" The Sheriff put his hand on Ryan's shoulder and steered him toward his office. When they were inside with the lights on the Sheriff said, "Let me see that cut on your chest." Ryan felt a surge of relief. *Someone's going to take care of me! Everything's going to be all right.* The Sheriff prodded at the cut and looked over Ryan's hands.

"I want to talk to my family," Ryan requested.

"Of course you do," he said. "I talked with your mother earlier today and I'm sorry to say that I talked her into staying at home until she heard from me again. I wasn't sure Jack's story would lead to anything." Ryan's heart fell at the prospect that his mom might have been on her way down if the sheriff hadn't talked her out of it. "Let's get you on the phone to your family and then I'll tend to your cuts and get something for you to wear."

Ryan had to free Lizzie Sue's hand from his, telling her he wouldn't leave her; he needed to make a phone call. Of course, Lizzie Sue had no idea what a phone call was, but she had enough to deal with just shielding her eyes from the brightness in the office. She looked up at Ryan and asked, "Phone call?"

None of this makes any sense to her, thought Ryan. *She's out of place here, just like I was on her mountain.* To Lizzie Sue he said, "Everything's going to be okay, I promise you. You'll be safe here. I'll stay with you Lizzie Sue as soon as I call my family." She dropped her hand and let it fall into her lap. The Sheriff took all this in.

Sheriff Martin turned the counter phone around so Ryan could use it. He picked it up and was surprised to find that he couldn't automatically remember his phone number and area code. When it came to him he punched in the numbers with his sore fingers and realized his whole body was shaking. He counted the rings, *One, two, three. What would they be doing right now,* he wondered. The clock above the desk said 2:13 a.m. *They'd be sleeping, of course. Four, come on, wake up Mom!* And then he heard her voice.

"We're coming Ryan. We're on our way. We left around 5:30 this afternoon. We love you! We love you!"

Ryan started to talk into the phone, before he realized it was not really his mom, just a recorded message. He listened to it with tears in his eyes and after the beep he whispered, "Please hurry!" He thought about hanging up and redialing so he could hear her voice again, but he put the phone down and told the sheriff that his family was already on their way. He went to Lizzie Sue and took her hand. His thoughts ran wild. *They're on their way. How? How did they know I was going to be here? Nobody knew I was getting away today except for Lizzie Sue. His tired mind couldn't figure it out.*

The Sheriff noticed how disoriented Ryan looked. He came over and held out a glass of water and a couple of doughnuts. "It's all I've got here, but you look like you could use it." He draped his coat around Ryan's shoulders and said, "When you've finished that I'll see to your cuts" Ryan had already guzzled the water.

"Thanks," said Ryan handing his glass back, "could I have more water? And Lizzie Sue might need some too." She shook her head no. She was confused and didn't trust her stomach to keep anything down. Ryan drained the second glass of water and devoured the doughnuts. The Sheriff took the glass and refilled it.

After the third glass of water the Sheriff came back with a first aid kit and some wet cloths. He really wanted to bring Ryan into a different room so he could clean him up better, but he knew the boy wanted to stay with the mountain woman. *There's something strange about this whole scene. If Ryan was kept against his will why is he being so protective of the woman? And if he wasn't kept against his will why didn't he come to town earlier? And how did he get that bruise on his cheek? First things first, I'll question him once his parents get here.*

Chapter 39

Jack, the deputy and Doc Tebo made their way up the trail. Doc was sixty-seven years old. Thick glasses covered his owlish green eyes. He had a bushy beard, a bulbous nose, professor eyebrows, and forty extra pounds on his frame. He wanted to retire, but the people of Mill Hollow hadn't been able to attract another doctor, so he was it. Of course, they could drive the hour to the next larger town over, but he'd been with these people his whole professional life and wouldn't desert them, not yet anyway.

Doc was used to late night emergency calls and just pulled his pants on over his pajamas. This was only the third time in over 40 years he'd been called in the middle of the night for a mountain person. They had their own ways and for the most part, the modern world left them alone and they left the modern world alone. There were 'healers' in the mountains that knew more about herbs and potions than he did, and these were the people they trusted when medical help was needed..

Doc's thoughts were broken by Jack's shouts, "There's the ledge." The deputy and Doc looked up where Jack had fixed the flashlight. They'd walked about a mile after parking the truck. Since this was his second drive up the mountain in one night with several treks up and down trails, the deputy wasn't happy to see the ledge was on an incline and at least six feet above their heads.

"Now how are we supposed ta get him down?" the deputy asked angrily. "If you had bothered ta tell us the ledge was so high up we coulda called in fer a hospital helicopter."

Doc broke in with, "What's done is done Earl, we need to deal with that man who's up there bleeding to death, or worse."

Jack was already thinking about how to get Amos down and had come up with a much lower tech idea. "If'n we kin git some ropes up there we kin lower him down."

"We've got ropes in the truck and a litter. I'll get them said the deputy," eager to trot back to the truck, if it meant he didn't have to hoist himself up that ledge. At the same time he was angry with himself for not bringing these things in the first place. Jack continued to search the area with his flashlight as he was formulating a plan. His thoughts were racing, *I don't have the book lairnin' those two do, but they sure ain't got the good sense God give 'em when it comes ta mountain ways. They're not gonna be much help but I owe it ta Amos and Lizzie Sue ta see ta gittin Amos some help.*

Jack took off his coat, folded it and laid it on the ground. He stood back looking at the ledge and judged the best spot to grab. He took a few steps back, ran and jumped higher than a man his size should have. He caught the ledge and slowly pulled himself up by his arms and sheer force of will. Doc Tebo was amazed at the man's agility. Once on the ledge Jack shook Amos, but there was no response. He felt Amos' body and it was cold, but not dead cold. Next he looked at the leg and Ryan's shirt wrapped around it. There was a lot of blood on that ledge.

By the time the deputy came back carrying rope and a portable litter Jack had been shouting down to Doc Tebo what little he could about Amos's condition. Doc, was pacing, anxious to get to his patient.

Huffing and puffing, the deputy tried to throw the rope up to Jack. He managed to get it near Jack on his fourth try. Jack shook his head and barked the rest of the instructions. "Tie the litter ta it and I'll haul it up. Then I'm gonna lower Amos down on the litter. Ye both be waitin' ta git him, he ain't a small man."

"How'll you get him down?" asked the deputy. "You can't do it by yourself." Doc Tebo didn't like letting Jack move Amos before he checked him but he saw no other way and they'd already wasted enough time.

Jack shook Amos once again, but there was no response. A few minutes later he felt a tug on the rope and he pulled up the litter. He untied it. Next he opened it and rolled Amos over onto it and then tied Amos and the litter together. He spoke out loud to Amos while he did this. "It's a good thin' yore knocked out Amos, cuz this is gonna hairt ye somethin' fierce."

Jack wrapped the rope twice around his own waist and then around his neck. He scooched Amos as close to the edge of the rock as possible. When he was sure he was ready he yelled to Doc and the deputy to get ready for Amos. With strength men half his age would have envied, Jack lowered Amos's body over the ledge and down the mountainside, using the rope around his body as leverage. He was letting the slack out as slowly as his hands allowed. Still, the rope cut into the flesh of his hands and his neck. He paid no attention, concentrating only on getting his neighbor help.

Doc Tebo watched the litter drop and bump against rocks and swing into the mountainside. It needed to come down another foot and he and Earl would be able to steady it. He worried that his patient, if he was still alive, might not make it through the rescue. The deputy broke Doc's concentration, "I don't know how that man is doing this." Amos' body inched closer to them and once it swung into reach, two pairs of hands grabbed the litter and lowered it to the ground. The deputy untied Amos, while Doc got busy assessing the man.

Up on the ledge Jack let out his last grunt and stumbled forward as he felt the weight hit the ground. He unwrapped the rope from his waist and yelled that it was coming down. He let the it drop and wiped the blood from his hands on his jeans. Without another thought about himself he began to lower himself over the ledge.

Doc started a portable IV for Amos and put an oxygen mask on his face. He checked Amos's vital signs and signaled to Earl and Jack to get his patient to the truck. Doc hurried after the litter and down the trail to the waiting truck. If the leg could be saved, and that was a big if, he was going to need months of physical therapy and rounds of antibiotics because of the exposed bone.

It was faster going down the trail than it had been coming up. Jack and the deputy settled Amos into the back of the truck and then Doc, with the help of Earl got in too. "Break all the rules getting us to town Earl if you want to give this man a fighting chance to keep his leg."

Jack shuddered at those words but he kept questions to himself. He worried about what was going to happen next. He knew he'd played a part in this unfolding drama, and right now he wasn't sure if he'd done the right thing. *What if*

Amos dies? What'll happen to Miz Lizzie? What if he lives and loses his leg? What's Becca thinkin' happened to me?

While the Sheriff was cleaning Ryan's wounds by first soaking and then wrapping his hands in gauze, Ryan was deep in thought and barely winced. Hearing his mom's voice on the answering machine stirred up conflicting emotions inside him. *What's going to happen to Lizzie Sue and Amos? What if Amos dies? Would it be his fault?*

The Sheriff left Ryan and the mountain woman alone after he'd done all he could for him. He knew Ryan would need professional care.

After the initial high from hearing his mom's voice and finding out they were on their way, his body crashed. The lights seemed artificially bright, his body hurt and he was confused by what was happening. Lizzie Sue leaned over to Ryan and said, "That man don't know nothin' bout how ta doctor. I kin help ye once we git Amos here." Ryan didn't even try to respond. Instead, he asked Lizzie Sue if she wanted some coffee. Feeling a bit calmer with Ryan at her side she nodded yes.

Ryan walked back to where the Sheriff was sitting and held up his bandaged hands. "Lizzie Sue would like some coffee and I can't get it for her." Sheriff Martin jumped up and reached for a cup. "She likes three spoons of sugar in it," Ryan added.

The Sheriff shook his head, "You seem to know a lot about her. Which makes me have questions for you, but I'm saving them until your parents get here. I shouldn't rightfully ask you too much without them present."

"That's okay," Ryan answered, as he followed the Sheriff back out to Lizzie Sue. He handed the cup to the woman who took it warily. But once it was in her hands she yelped.

"Take it back Ryan, it's gonna melt in my hands!" The sheriff took it back from her, spilling some on the floor in the process, but it was Ryan who answered her.

"It's a Styrofoam cup. It won't melt, it's really strong. People use them instead of china cups."

"Cain't the Sheriff afford no china cups?"

Ryan smiled at this and realized it felt good to smile. "People use these cups so they don't have to wash them. They just throw them away."

Lizzie Sue shook her head. "Seems not right ta throw thin's like that out." Ryan watched Lizzie Sue gingerly take the coffee back. She took a sip and kept her thoughts about the taste of it to herself.

Ryan sat back and rested his head against the wall. "Would you like to lay down on one of the cots in the cell? They're both empty," said the Sheriff, nodding with his head to the jail cells. Even though his body ached to lie down and just sleep he shook his head and said he'd wait with Lizzie Sue. "Let me know if you change your mind." He glanced at the clock, which said 3:07 a.m. "Doc and Earl should be back soon."

"Where's Pa," asked Lizzie Sue with tears in her eyes.

"He'll be here soon and we'll get him to a hospital."

"Hospital?" Lizzie Sue asked.

Ryan shook his head. He kept forgetting, that despite her age, Lizzie Sue was like a small child when it came to the modern world. "A hospital is where there are lots of doctors with good medicine. They'll help Amos get better there."

"I kin git him better Ryan. Jist like I did fer ye. I got my herbs jist waitin' back home."

"I don't think you can get him better this time Lizzie Sue, not with any herbs you take out of your bag."

"Is he hairt that bad?"

"He's hurt pretty bad, but I think it's mostly hi..." Ryan's sentence was cut off by the scream of a siren and flashing lights coming toward them.

Lizzie Sue jumped up and clamped her hands over her ears. "Lord help us!" she shouted looking toward heaven. She started jerking around, looking for a place to hide. Then her eyes caught on the red flashing lights, which appeared outside the window where she was standing. Finally, there was silence and Lizzie Sue plopped back in her chair, clearly shaken. Ryan was unnerved by Lizzie Sue's reaction too. Now that she was back in her chair he tried to explain the sound was the siren on an ambulance, which would take Amos to the hospital.

"He won't like it," she answered. "He don't want me off'n the mountain."

"He probably won't even know you're here. At least not right away because he's hurt that bad," Ryan explained.

"Oh, oh, oh." She moaned softly, rocking herself back and forth and letting silent tears fall. Ryan's heart broke for this woman but all he could do was wait with her and feel guilty that he was the one who'd started this chain of events by chasing an eagle.

Ryan's weariness took over and he leaned his head back against the wall and closed his eyes, his head coming to rest on Lizzie Sue's shoulder. The woman waited about ten minutes before she allowed herself to reach up and stroke Ryan's face. The Sheriff watched her from behind the counter, sipping his own cup of coffee. He shook his head as he walked back to his office to wait for Earl and Doc's return with the mountain man.

Slamming car doors startled Ryan awake. He looked around expecting to find himself in the small loft bedroom on the mountain. Instead he was greeted with bright lights, a stiff neck and the fear in Lizzie Sue's eyes.

"Amos must be here," said Ryan rubbing his neck. He glanced at the clock, it was 3:29. *Or maybe it's my parents!* he thought with lightness in his heart. He peered out the window and saw it was the deputy. He took Lizzie Sue's hand the best he could with his bandages and said a silent prayer on the way outside.

The two ambulance drivers rechecked Amos' vital signs. Doc Tebo assisted and gave directions. The image Lizzie Sue saw of her husband was of a pale man with a white sheet pulled up to his neck and a clear mask of some kind over his face, a needle was stuck in his arm with other fancy gadgets attached to him. "Amos, Amos, kin ye hear me?" She looked around frantically. "I need my doctorin' bag Ryan. Ye got ta git it fer me!" Ryan didn't know what to say. He pulled Lizzie Sue away with his bandaged hands and winced at the pain that shot through his fingers.

"We need to get out of the way and let these people help Amos." She watched him being put in the back end of the car with flashing lights and bit her knuckles. "They cain't jist take Pa like that!" She grabbed hold of Ryan's arm and squeezed. "He needs some of my special tea, he's too peaked. He'll need at least two strong cups. I cain't tell what else until I lay my hands on him." Ryan remained quiet, watching the paramedics shut the door of the ambulance. Jack shook his head and rubbed his neck. He was going to be sore tomorrow.

Doc Tebo spoke up, "I'm going with you, this man's in bad shape."

"I have ta be with Pa, he needs me!" Lizzie Sue looked directly into Ryan's eyes and then into Jack's. She was perfectly willing to get into the same vehicle that just a few minutes ago had scared her.

"Are ye sure ye want ta do that Miz Lizzie?" asked Jack who really didn't want to go to the hospital because he wanted to get home to Becca.

Ryan felt torn. Surely his family would be here soon, but how could he let Lizzie Sue do this alone? She couldn't even read, she didn't know about anything that would be happening to Amos. "I'll go with you," he finally said.

Jack countered with, "Well if ye think that's best, I'll let ye take care a Miz Lizzie and I'll be gittin' on home." He was glad to be let off the hook and was thinking he'd check in with the Sheriff again when he came down in a week or so to get the winter staples he'd meant to get today.

Doc Tebo shouted, "Well get in if you're coming! We're wasting time and this man doesn't have much of it.

"Tell my parents to meet me at the hospital," Ryan yelled to the Sheriff as he crawled into the back of the ambulance.

The Sheriff shook his head and ran back toward his truck. "I'm right behind you!" He shouted back to the deputy, "Wait for Mr. and Mrs. Burns and explain what happened. Send them on to the hospital."

The deputy went back inside the office, scratching his head. *How can I explain any of this ta that kid's parents? It's the strangest case of kidnapping I've ever seen.* With the darkest part of the night long over Earl didn't think he'd be getting to bed any time soon, so he sat back in the chair, put his legs up on the desk, rested his head on the back of the chair and waited for the Burn's family.

On the ride to the hospital Ryan asked Doc Tebo if the sirens could be turned off. He explained that they frightened Lizzie Sue. "Is this her first time off the mountain?" asked Doc Tebo. Ryan nodded yes and Doc continued, "Poor thing, she's got some unpleasantness ahead of her." Ryan said nothing, but stared at Lizzie Sue who was speaking softly to her husband and gently probing his body to find out how he was doing. Doc warned her to stay away from the legs. She uncovered Amos and moaned softly when she saw the bone.

Going at the best speed possible it took 45-mintues to get to Mercy Hospital. Amos was whisked away to surgery while Doc Tebo filled in the waiting surgical team, who'd been called in to work on Amos. He was reluctant to give up his patient, but stopped at the doors to the operating room. Ryan tried as best he could to explain to Lizzie Sue about surgery and why she couldn't go with Amos.

In the Sheriff's office Lizzie Sue was still close to her mountain. She could see it from the window. But here in a new town, in a hospital where everything was bright and modern, things were different. Ryan led her to a waiting room. She sat in the soft chair for a moment and then got back up and touched the hallway floor. Everything was so shiny she thought it was wet, like after a rain. In spite of the situation Ryan smiled at Lizzie Sue.

She came back to the waiting room and wrapped her shawl close around her, not because she was cold, but because she felt foreign and out of place, and wanted to look as small as she could. Her lace-up boots, long skirt and hand-sewn blouse weren't anything like the clothes she saw as she looked around. Most people wore white or light green and since it was bright everywhere she looked, she felt a headache coming on.

Ordinarily Lizzie Sue never thought about her looks. Her clothes were made to be sturdy and practical, and her appearance was never of any concern to her. Seeing the strange clothes, watching people take Pa away, feeling her raw nerves and the brightness of the surroundings around her, left her disoriented. Ryan wondered if she was going into shock. He kept her hand wrapped around his arm and chatted with her.

After a few minutes at the front desk the Sheriff escorted Ryan and Lizzie Sue to the admitting desk. "They'll need to ask you some questions about Amos." Then he left to get a cup of coffee and secure a ride home for Doc Tebo.

The nurse looked at Lizzie Sue like she was something the cat dragged in, and pushed a pen, clipboard, and several sheets of white paper toward her. "Fill these out over there," said the nurse, pointing to the waiting area. "Bring them back to the desk when you're done."

Lizzie Sue looked at Ryan, her eyes wide. Ryan looked at his bandaged hands and told Lizzie Sue to bring everything with her and that he and the Sheriff would help fill them out. They waited quietly for Sheriff Martin to come back, and when he did Ryan asked him to write for Lizzie Sue. "She can't read or write, and I can't write either," Ryan said, holding up his hurt hands.

"Tell you what, you go in the bathroom over there and change into this shirt I got from the nurses." Ryan was still wearing the Sheriff's coat. "When you bring back my coat we'll fill these forms out together. Ryan looked at Lizzie Sue and the Sheriff saw his concern. "Don't worry Ryan, I won't leave her." Ryan let out a breath and started for the bathroom. Sheriff Martin watched him go and marveled at the strong and loving spirit this young boy had.

About thirty minutes after the ambulance left Mill Hollow for Mercy Hospital the Burns' car screeched to a halt in front of the Sheriff's office. Ted tried to give a last warning to his wife, but she was out of the car and in the office, talking to the deputy faster than he could finish what he wanted to say.

"Is he here? Where's Ryan?"

Earl jumped up and extended his hand, which Sarah ignored. "No," he said. "I mean he's not here right now, but yes, he's alive."

"Where is he?" demanded Ted.

"He's with the Sheriff over at Mercy Hospital."

"What's wrong with him? Why's he in the hospital?" worried Sarah.

"No, no, no," Deputy Earl said, holding up his hands as if to fend off anymore questions. "I'm not explaining myself real good here. Yer son is fine, but come in ta the Sheriff's office and I'll explain some things ta ye."

"We don't need explanations," shouted Sarah, "we need directions." She grabbed at Ben's hand and turned to Ted. "Get the directions Ted, we'll be waiting in the car."

The deputy spoke faster, "Really Mrs. Burns, there are some things ye should know before ye go ta the hospital." Sarah thought she'd explode. She needed to see her son now!

"Come on Mom," said Ben. "Let's not argue. Listen to what the deputy has to say, and then we'll go to the hospital." He was buzzing inside with good feelings about Ryan so he knew his twin was safe.

The Sheriff put A-M-O-S above the box marked first name. He was going to need Ryan's help to fill out anything else. Ryan returned looking a little better in a shirt that was only a couple sizes too big, instead of the bigger, bulkier coat he'd been wearing. "Son, do you know Amos's last name?"

"Riley," answered Ryan as he settled into the spot next to Lizzie Sue, who immediately tucked her arm back through his.

"I'm sure Amos doesn't have a social security number," said the Sheriff, but what about any kind of address?" Ryan suggested that he put on the tallest mountain above Mill Hollow. The Sheriff went on, "I know he hasn't got any insurance."

That was when something snapped inside Ryan's head, *Insurance? How are Lizzie Sue and Amos going to pay for all of this? Surgery and blood transfusions and ambulance rides would cost thousands of dollars.* " Ryan's heart sank, *What has my selfish idea of finding the eagle's nest, cost everyone – Mom, Dad, Ben, Lizzie Sue, Amos?* That June morning seemed a lifetime ago. He hardly listened as the Sheriff asked him other questions about Amos. The Sheriff finally gave up shaking his head and realized there was nothing more they could answer on the forms. Before he left to bring them back to the admitting nurse he asked Lizzie Sue if she could sign her name as next of kin.

"I kin make the first part of it, Ryan was gonna lairn me how ta do it, but things went fast after I brung the bible out and realized he knew all them words." This didn't make much sense to the sheriff but he handed her the pen and pointed to where she should write her name. Lizzie Sue was momentarily amazed at it and asked how it got sharpened. Ryan laughed and told her a pen was different than a pencil and never needed sharpening. With this explanation, which she didn't understand, she scrawled a childish LIZ on the paper and gave everything back to the Sheriff.

Once the Sheriff was gone Lizzie Sue whispered to Ryan, "Where's the privy?"

Ryan stammered around before answering her, "Well, there aren't any privies down here." He noticed the anguished look on Lizzie Sue's face and realized she had taken what he said wrong. He tried again, "What I mean, is that they're inside the buildings. I'll show you where one is." He got off the couch, but Lizzie Sue stayed sitting with a dumbfounded look on her face. "What's wrong?" Ryan asked.

Lizzie Sue gestured for Ryan to bend down, which he did, grimacing at the pain in his muscles. "How do they git rid a the stink in there? she whispered.

Ryan laughed, he laughed so hard that tears started rolling down his cheeks. He flopped back onto the couch and continued laughing. Lizzie Sue started chuckling and then let out some real snorts, not knowing what she was laughing at, but feeling some of her tension ease. Sheriff Martin walked over to them and smiled at what he saw. "What's going on here?" he asked.

Ryan wiped his face with his gauzed hands and got up again. Lizzie Sue got up this time too. "I'm just going to show her where the bathroom is." Ryan tried his best to explain bathrooms and flushing to Lizzie Sue before she went in. He was kind of embarrassed, but knew she needed some help. "I'll wait right here for you. *This must be how parents feel when they let their kids go to a public restroom by themselves for the first time.*

He looked at his watch, 4:35. *What's taking mom and dad so long?*

After a few minutes Lizzie Sue popped her small head out the door. She looked a little puzzled. "Ryan, is that smooth, shiny thin' above the water that comes out of that little tiny faucet a big mirror jist like the itty bitty one I got in my under the bed box?"

"Yeah, that's a mirror."

"That must cost a lot a money for one a them." Lizzie Sue shook her head.

"You mean you've never seen your whole self in a mirror before?"

"Well least ways not one as big as that. Why would a body want to look at thereself while they's washin' up?"

"I've never really thought about it before, but it's a good question."

When they got back to the waiting room the only other person there was the Sheriff. "Here's something else that will amaze you Lizzie Sue." Ryan awkwardly turned on the TV set which was situated in the corner of the waiting room. It blared to life showing a picture of an old western where cowboys were branding cows. Ryan turned to look at her face as he slowly flipped the channels one after another, forgetting about the pain in his hands. Lizzie Sue walked over to the TV and touched the screen with her hand. Then she looked behind the TV and under it.

"It's called a television Lizzie Sue, and don't ask me how they get the picture in there because I don't understand it either. Do you want me to leave it on or turn it off?"

"Kin ye git it back ta the place where them big fish was swimmin' in all that water?"

"They're called whales," Ryan informed her as he flipped the channels again until he came to the Discovery Channel. "This used to be one of my favorite channels too."

"What do ye do with all them pictures?" wondered Lizzie Sue.

"You just watch them. You don't really do anything with them. It's just for fun and for learning." Lizzie Sue couldn't take her eyes away from the beautiful whales.

Chapter 40

Sheriff Martin paced back and forth. He had just finished talking to Earl and he knew that the Burns' family was on their way here. He thought about telling Ryan, but the boy was momentarily dozing on the woman's shoulder again. *He probably needs looking after by a doctor too, but I'll let his family make that decision.* He snuck a peak at the mountain woman and Ryan. She was patting his leg and humming softly.

About twenty minutes later Ryan was awakened by a flurry of activity in the room. He jumped up; feeling more clear-headed than he had in a long time, and knew his brother was close. He looked around the waiting room. His heart raced and he realized he was holding his breath.

"Ryan!" He didn't know who said it, and it didn't matter.

"Here! I'm Here!" he shouted as he followed the voices.

His mom got to him before the others, hugging him hard and crying and then touching his face, the scar on his forehead, his hair, and his bandaged hands, and then hugging him again. Ryan didn't even notice the hugs hurt his raw chest; he was with his family again. His dad wrapped his arms around both of them and Ben dove in for the old Burns' family hug. Ryan was laughing and crying and trying to talk all at once. Ben kept his arm around Ryan while his dad broke away to blow his nose. The nurses and a few doctors, who'd been alerted by the Sheriff as to what was happening,

218

stopped to stare at the touching reunion, and spontaneously began clapping.

Ben thought he would burst. He felt so whole and connected again that he didn't want to take his eyes off his twin. He noted that Ryan's hair *was* as long as his, although not nearly as neat and clean. *We'll have to decide later,* he thought, *after I fill Ryan in about dad having a ponytail, whether we want to keep our hair this long, or get it cut.*

Lizzie Sue was taking in the reunion and had tears of her own streaming down her face. She didn't know that Ryan had an identical twin and was momentarily jealous of the woman who got to keep two boys who looked so much like Charlie. Lizzie Sue knew she was losing another son for good, and now turned her thoughts to Amos. *I need ta see him. Where is he?* She wanted to ask Ryan but knew it wasn't her place to intrude on the family reunion.

Sarah couldn't keep her hands off Ryan and he didn't mind. Just when she thought she had her crying under control she'd start up again. A nurse brought more tissues, which were filling up Sarah's purse.

Finally Ryan felt the tug of Lizzie Sue's love and realized she must be feeling terrible with all this hugging going on. He broke away from his family to go to her. Sarah noticed how gently Ryan tended to the mountain woman and knew her son felt something for this woman, something similar but different to what he felt for her. She looked over at Ted and the Sheriff who were engaged in a heated argument and thought, *Why can't Ted just be happy that we've got Ryan back? Nothing else matters now! We're whole and our life can begin again!*

219

Ted stormed over to his family with the Sheriff close behind. "Mom, Dad, Ben," said Ryan, "you haven't met Lizzie Sue."

"No, and I don't want to!" yelled Ted. Ryan looked at his dad, puzzled by his attitude until he heard the Sheriff talking to Lizzie Sue.

"I'm sorry I have to do this, Ma'am, but I have to take you back to Mill Hollow."

"But what about Pa? He needs me here!" Lizzie Sue was wide-eyed and frightened and looked toward Ryan.

"I know Ma'am, but what you and yer husband did to Ryan was wrong. Mr. Burns is pressing charges. I need to take you to jail. Listen to me carefully now." The Sheriff's voice was low and soothing. He knelt on one leg before Lizzie Sue, and held one of her hands, looking like he was proposing marriage to her. He continued, "I'm arresting you for the kidnapping of Ryan Burns. You have the right to remain silent. You have the right to an attorney. If you cannot afford an attorney, one will be provided for you. Anything you say can, and will, be used against you in a court of law." Lizzie Sue didn't understand all the big words and looked at the sheriff like a bewildered child.

Ryan couldn't believe what he was hearing. *Hadn't everybody suffered enough? Amos was paying a price right now up in surgery, and Lizzie Sue hadn't done anything except take care of him.* Lizzie Sue's voice interrupted his thoughts.

"Ryan, what do all them words mean?"

Ryan ignored her question and turned to his dad. "Dad, you can't do this to her!" he screamed.

220

"I can and I have. All we need is to stop back at Mill Hollow to fill out some forms and then we'll be on our way. If I never see this place again it'll be fine with me!"

Ryan stamped his foot, "Dad, you don't understand!"

"No! You don't understand Ryan. Do you know what these people have put your mother through?" Ted's voice cracked and he looked to Sarah for support. She looked down at her hands.

"Lizzie Sue needs to be with Amos," Ryan persisted. "She doesn't even know if he's going to live or die. How can you be so mean? They need each other now more than ever."

"You think *I'm* being mean? I'm the only one doing what's right here."

"You have no right to come down here and throw her in jail, Dad. I'm waiting with her until Amos is out of surgery." Ryan fought to gain control over his shaking voice.

The Sheriff broke in, "Can we all please just sit down and wait?" Five pairs of eyes were on Ted. He threw up his arms and walked away. The Sheriff gave Lizzie Sue's hand a pat and stood up.

Sarah sat on the other side of Ryan, each woman had one of his arms wrapped around her own. Ben sat on the floor in front of Ryan and leaned up against his twin. Ryan felt cocooned in love, and wished his dad would come sit too.

After a few minutes Sarah asked, "Ryan what's wrong with your hands?"

"They're just hurt from climbing down the mountain. They'll be okay." Then she noticed scratches rising up from under the shirt.

"I think we should have a doctor look at you while we wait for Amos to get out of surgery."

"Later mom, I just want to sit here with all of you for a while. The sheriff looked at me, I'm fine." Sarah let it go, she could see he was in no immediate danger, and wasn't really anxious to let a doctor take him away. She sat back again, wanting to hear more of the story, but sensing this wasn't the right time to ask questions. She had a whole lifetime ahead of her to catch up on what had happened to her son the last few months. For now she told herself she was content just to sit next to him.

The next hour and a half was tense. Ryan continued to sit between Lizzie Sue and his mom, but it was his mother's shoulder that Ryan's head rested against. Ben tried more than anyone to keep the conversation going. He talked about school and people they knew, but after a while it began to sound hollow, since he hadn't exactly been hanging around with their old friends anyway.

Finally, a young surgeon came in to give them a report: they'd been able to save Amos's leg, although he was likely to be left with a limp and would need physical therapy. He'd lost lots of blood and had to have a transfusion. There had been some internal bleeding, and he also had a concussion, but all in all, the doctor said he was lucky to be alive. "It's probably his rugged life in the mountains that kept him in good enough shape to get through this ordeal."

Ryan hugged Lizzie Sue and his dad watched them. "Does that mean Pa'll be okay?"

"Yes, he'll be fine," answered Ryan. "But it will take a long time for him to get better."

"Kin I see him?"

"Yes Ma'am," the doctor answered. "He's in room 224. He's still pretty groggy but he'll be glad to see you. Keep in mind that he'll be a little disoriented from the concussion, but that will pass."

Just wait until he really wakes up, thought Ryan. *He won't know where he is and he'll have to get used to losing his son again.* Ryan turned to talk to his family. In a calm voice, much more in charge and confident than they'd heard before, he said, "I'm going to take Lizzie Sue to see Amos."

"We'll go with you honey," suggested Sarah. She'd just gotten him back and wasn't about to let him out of her sight for even a minute. All of them trooped onto an elevator. It was a strange mix of people, Sheriff Martin, a small mountain woman, twin boys, one of whom had bandaged hands and dirty clothes. Then there were Sarah and Ted, standing as far apart as the elevator allowed.

Lizzie Sue's eyes widened at the closing of the doors and the moving room where everyone just stood still. Once on the second floor Ryan took Lizzie Sue to room 224. He asked her if she wanted to go in alone or with him. He thought about all of the tubes and other things that were probably hooked up to Amos and how they might scare her. But she decided to go in alone. Ryan felt proud of her as she entered the room. Sarah said a silent prayer for this woman who had taken care of her son. She knew she'd never be able to repay her.

Lizzie Sue stood about a foot away from Amos and studied him. His eyes were closed. He was wearing a nightshirt with little blue designs on it. His color wasn't good she noted, but she knew that some fennel tea would fix that right up. Next, she looked at the bag of bright red blood hooked up to him and some other bag with clear liquid in it. She wasn't sure what to make of that so she went next to his leg. It was encased in a big white, hard thing and there were more tubes coming out of it.

Now she was ready to do her own doctoring. She started at his head and began to probe for any unusual bumps. Amos awoke with the familiar touch. "Ma!" he moaned.

"I'm here Pa. Jist ye be still now."

"Charlie? Is Charlie okay? Where's Charlie?"

Ryan stood just outside the door. He watched Lizzie Sue tense slightly at the mention of Charlie.

"Charlie's gone Pa. He's up with the angels."

"Ye mean I couldn't save him, Ma?"

"No, Pa, he's gone. Ye did yer best, but Charlie's gone fer good. When ye git home I'll show ye where we buried him." Lizzie Sue held his big hand in both of her small ones and watched her man grieve for the son he lost yet again.

"What's gonna happen to them Sheriff?" asked Ryan.

"A lot of that depends on your dad, son."

Mr. Burns looked at the couple in room 224 and shook his head. "You don't understand Ryan. You feel sorry for them now, but that was us crying for you over the last few months. They deserve to be punished. What they did was wrong!"

Ryan shook his head and looked at the floor, but when he spoke his voice was under control. "If it weren't for Lizzie Sue and Amos I would have died out there on that mountain. If anyone's to blame for all of this," Ryan looked up and opened his arms to gesture at the whole scene, "it's me! Please, Dad, I want to go home. I want to pick up where we left off and we can do that. It won't be as easy for Amos and Lizzie Sue."

Ted was tired. Tired of driving. Tired of holding back his emotions to stay strong for his family, but above all, he was tired of fighting. He looked directly at Ryan and knew his son needed to win this argument. "You like these people? You don't want me to press charges?" Ryan shook his head. "Fine, we'll let it be your call." Ted's hands, which had been stabbing the air to punctuate his words, now fell in surrender to his side. Ryan's smile brightened the whole room as he moved toward his dad to hug him.

Next Ryan turned his attention to the Sheriff and asked him who would take care of Lizzie Sue until Amos got better.

"Don't worry about that son. Jack's decided to split the reward money with Amos and Lizzie Sue. My wife and I'll make sure she's taken care of until they get back up the mountain."

Ted opened his mouth to object, it was his money that would be going to these people, but he closed it as fast as he'd opened it. *I can't put a price on my son.* He put a hand on both of his sons' shoulders and said, "Let's get going. We're not stopping until we're out of this state!" Ted began herding his family toward the elevator."

"I'll be right with you, Dad," announced Ryan. "Hold the elevator for me."

"Ryan!" yelled his dad, but it was his mom who followed him back to room 224. She stood at the door while her son said his good-byes to the people who had kept him from his family.

Amos was sleeping again, which Ryan thought was just as well. He told Lizzie Sue that the Sheriff would help her out. He gave her a hug and then slipped off his watch and put it on her. "Think of me when you wear this, Lizzie Sue. I'll think of you every time I see this scar on my head." He fingered the welt she had sewn up for him. Ryan gave Lizzie Sue a hug and she hung onto him, not wanting to let go. Sarah dabbed at the tears in her eyes and realized this woman and her son had gone through a lot together. She thanked God for the motherly love in Lizzie Sue's heart.

Ryan turned to go and saw that his mom had followed him and witnessed what had just taken place. He wiped a tear from his face. She offered him her arm and he linked his with hers, allowing himself to be led to the elevator where the rest of his family was waiting for him.

"It seems like we have a lot to talk about," said Sarah.

Ryan acknowledged this with a nod of his head. "I'll tell you all about it Mom, I promise, but not right now. Let's just get in the car. I'm starved. Can we stop at McDonalds?" Sarah laughed, knowing that he was still the same Ryan, deep down to the pit of his stomach.

Epilogue

It was mid-July when Jack came riding by Amos and Lizzie Sue's house. He had his wife and eight month old daughter with him. Amos came out to meet them. He walked with a pronounced limp, but it didn't keep him from life as usual on the mountain.

Lizzie Sue held her arms out for the baby and Becca handed her down. "Me and the family was inta town last week and the Sheriff give us a package for ye. He says it's fer Miz Lizzie." He took the package off the wagon and brought it into the house.

Lizzie Sue, who had never gotten a package like this before, admired the stamps and neat writing. She noticed it said LIZ. She untied the string, being careful not to hurt it since it would come in handy later on. Next she folded the brown paper and finally opened the box. It contained some coffee and sugar, a large tablet of paper and a box of colored pencils and pens. Digging further she found three bars of green soap, wool socks, a small pair and a big pair. There were also some lemon drops, yarn, and a few magazines with lots of pictures, a small mirror, and some mints. A large picture book of whales lay on top of two old white sheets, which were neatly pressed and folded at the bottom of the box. When she took them out she found an envelope, with a school picture of Ryan, which she carefully put in her pocket before Pa saw it. It would hide in there next to the watch that she always carried with her.

She unfolded a piece of paper from the envelope and saw a picture of a whale beautifully drawn and colored. She knew it was from Ryan.

"Who would send them things to ye, Ma?" inquired Amos.

"I 'spect it's someone I met while ye was in the hospital when ye was sick, Pa. Ye don't know him." She winked at Jack as she caressed the watch in her pocket, a thing she did dozens of times throughout the day.

THE END

QUESTIONS
FOR
EAGLE ROCK

Questions for Eagle Rock

1. Compare and contrast the two main families in Eagle Rock: the Burns' and the Riley's.

2. Loss is a theme in Eagle Rock. How many forms of loss can you name from this book?

3. Lizzie Sue Riley and Sarah Burns are two very different women. Which mother did you relate to? Why?

4. What problems do you think Ryan and Ben will encounter as they try to reclaim their life as eighth graders?

5. Do you think living with Ryan helped Lizzie Sue deal with the death of her own son, or do you think it made it worse for her? Why?

6. The mothers were stronger characters than the fathers in Eagle Rock. Do you think this is true in real life? Explain.

7. Explain which member of the Burns' family you think handled stress the best.

8. Which character do you think changed the most during the story? How did he or she change?

9. Which character would you like to be? Why?

10. Do you think Ryan should have tried to escape earlier from Amos and Lizzie Sue? How would he have done this?

11. What were the ways that Ben put his life on hold until his twin returned?

12. How would this story have changed if Jack had not seen Ryan?

13. During the time that Ryan was lost and wandering in the mountains what do you think he did right? What do you think he did wrong?

14. Why doesn't Lizzie Sue show Amos the picture of Ryan?

15. The book covers only 117 days but the last third of the book takes place in less than a day. Why do you think the author used time in this way?